CW01374258

RIGGS

STARGAZER ALIEN MAIL ORDER BRIDES (BOOK 15)

TASHA BLACK

RIGGS

SAGE

In her dream, Sage emerged from the rubble.

She had no memory of how she had gotten here. There was only the scent of charred wood and the thunderous echo of a recent explosion in her ears.

Instinctively, she knew the way to safety was forward, but she was looking out over a sea of jagged rock and splintered wood.

She gazed down at her bare feet, then spun around, hoping to find another way out.

A fog of dust hung thick in the air behind her. Whatever had just happened was back there. Forward was the only way.

Sage took a deep breath and stepped into the rubble.

She gasped, not from the pain she expected, but from surprise.

The jagged rocks beneath her feet somehow felt smooth as sand.

Sage was a logical person. Frantically, her mind grasped at reasons she wasn't feeling pain. Maybe she was in shock from whatever had happened just outside the reach of her memory. Maybe she'd had nerve damage.

But as her mind worked, her feet blithely navigated the rocky terrain, carrying her further from the cloud of dust and closer to something that pulled at her like a magnet.

A wall of golden yellow and emerald green began to emerge out of the mist before her.

And the shape of someone, looming before it, wide shouldered and frightening.

She couldn't turn back or even pause her trek. He drew her in, like a vortex.

Sage blinked the dust out of her eyes as her feet carried her closer still.

The shadowy figure took on depth and reality hit Sage like a kick to the chest.

It was Riggs standing before her.

Of course it was.

The hunky alien invaded all her dreams lately, insinuating himself into her every nightmare and saving the day with a smoldering look or gesture.

He didn't confine himself to her dreams either. Riggs was constantly underfoot in real life too, trying to help her around the farm, but mostly just distracting her with his beguiling scent and his excessively muscular body.

He wasn't exactly a chatterbox, thankfully. But the intense look in his blue eyes told her he wanted her more than his words ever could.

Sage wasn't used to being the object of so much pent-up passion. She hadn't done much dating - her life had mainly revolved around her education and keeping an eye on her impulsive younger sister. She'd always assumed she'd meet a nice guy in grad school with similar interests and that would be that.

Riggs was many things, but he wasn't a nice guy.

Not because he wasn't nice, but rather that he wasn't a guy at all, really. He was an alien.

Besides, no nice guy could look like he did - all bristling muscles, angled cheekbones and icy blue eyes.

And he was an impossible distraction from the enormous task of running the farm and organizing the books.

At least here in the dream she could safely succumb to temptation.

This will get it out of your system. Kiss him once and call me in the morning.

But melting into his arms didn't feel like medicine.

Dream-Riggs was looking down at her, jaw tense, lightning flashing in his eyes.

She moved closer and he extended his hand to touch her cheek. Sage gasped at the shiver of pleasure that ran to her core at this gentle touch. It felt real, so real.

He bent to kiss her.

Sage went up on her toes, sliding her hands up his biceps as she longed to do in real life. Each of his arms was as broad as one of the young peach trees on the hillside of the farm.

He flexed and the muscles rolled under her hands.

Sage bit back a moan as his lips hit hers and she lost herself to the ecstasy of his embrace.

He ran his hands through her hair and she could feel the tilt and spin of the Earth, the eternity of the stars.

Sage...

The universe seemed to call her name.

Sage.

"Sage," the masculine voice came from just outside her bedroom door.

It wasn't Riggs.

She opened her eyes to greet the day, such as it was. The pink of dawn hadn't lit her windows yet.

But she always got up early.

Apparently someone else got up even earlier.

"Just a minute," she called out softly.

She slid out of bed and wrapped a robe around her before opening the door.

Otis Rogers stood on the other side, shifting the weight of his heavy frame from one leg to the other anxiously.

Not the man she was hoping to see.

You are not hoping to see any man show up outside your bedroom door. Nothing good can come of that.

Maybe *something* could.

"I'm really, really sorry to wake you," Otis said. "Arden told me you're usually up at five."

"Five-fifteen," Sage said. "What do you need?"

"I just wondered if it was okay for me to use the last of the unsalted butter," he said.

"It's fine," she said. "Go ahead and use it."

His wide face broke into a sunny grin.

"Thank you," he said.

He gave her a little wave and went back down the hallway toward the kitchen. Sage shook her head, wondering when he would feel his debt to the family was paid.

Otis had been part of a scheme to steal the bees from their farm, sabotaging their peach crop. He had confessed and was apparently trying to work off his guilt by baking for them. A lot.

Sage got up early each morning, but couldn't imagine being up early enough to arrive at someone else's house before dawn without invitation or payment.

She headed to the bathroom to grab a quick shower and get ready for the day.

The dream still clung to the edges of her mind.

Get with the program, Sage.

With luck, she could pull herself together enough not to still be daydreaming about Riggs when he appeared in real life.

The shower didn't help.

Somehow the hot water pounding her skin only made her think of his warm mouth on hers. She closed her eyes and pictured his hands instead of her own sliding the soap all over her.

Enough, Sage, she told herself, opening her eyes. *You have work to do.*

She rinsed off as quickly as she could, got dressed and headed to the kitchen.

Sage had taken over cooking duty when she and Tansy moved to the farm after Grandma Helen's funeral. The days on the farm were long, with so much manual labor that she was amazed Helen had been able to accomplish it all right up until the end, even with a few farmhands. Sage liked to start the day with a hearty breakfast.

Now that Arden and the three alien men from the lab next door had joined them, meal prep was literally three times as much work. Honestly, probably five times as much, given the way the men ate.

But Sage couldn't complain, the three fugitive aliens worked as hard as any ten men and Arden's background in botany had already gotten them out of one major jam. Not to mention that Sage enjoyed her company. It had been a while since she had a true friend that wasn't her sister.

They had a good thing going.

Except for all the mating.

First Arden and Drago had paired up, and then her sister Tansy had bonded with Burton. Now everyone was looking expectantly at Sage and Riggs.

Well it wasn't going to happen. Sage had plenty to keep her busy. She wasn't going to waste her time falling in love, especially with an alien. She had promised her little sister that they would try to save the farm. With everyone else distracted, Sage needed to stay sober and focused.

The hallways leading to the kitchen smelled heavenly.

When she arrived she nearly wept.

Otis was bent over the stove to remove a tray of croissants. The kitchen table was already practically groaning under the weight of two massive coffee cakes, a tray of homemade doughnuts and a pastry ring of some kind.

Dirty dishes were stacked on every counter top and the whole kitchen looked as if there had been a light snow. Sage presumed it was flower, or confectioners' sugar. Probably both.

It was a mountain of carbohydrates and mess, without a gram of protein to carry a farmer through a long day's work.

"Think this is enough?" Otis asked over his shoulder.

"Um, yes," Sage replied. She was going to have the devil of a time cleaning the kitchen.

"There's coffee on the picnic table," Otis said. "Why don't you have a cup while I clean up in here?"

She almost refused and then she remembered that he had tried to sabotage the farm. Besides, she was pretty sure he wasn't actually going to get the kitchen cleaned up - at least not to her standards.

"Thanks," she said. "I think I will."

She stepped outside.

The first pink rays of dawn peeked over the hillside to greet her.

True to his word, Otis had placed a tray of mugs and milk along with the coffee carafe on the picnic table under the magnolia tree.

Sage grabbed a mug and poured herself a steaming helping of the brew. The farm was so quiet and lovely early in the morning. She had to admit it was nice to relax for a moment before the bustle of the day began.

And to get her thoughts together before she saw Riggs.

2

RIGGS

R iggs looked out over Martin's Bounty Farm from the top of a thirty-foot ladder.

He had planned to be up early so he could help Sage with kitchen duty. But he had awoken earlier than planned and decided to tackle another item on the list of things to be done on the farm.

He had chosen to hang the signs on the barn that advertised the fact the peaches were in season and ready to be picked.

It had seemed like a simple enough task from the ground. He climbed the ladder with relative ease, and hung the beautiful hand-painted sign.

Welcome to Martin's Bounty
Pick-Your-Own-Peaches Season is Here!

BUT ONCE HE was up so high, Riggs found himself hypnotized by the view.

The berry fields stretched out below and the tree line between the Martins' land and Dolly Strickland's farm looked less defined than it did from the ground. His eye traced the path of the paved road curving toward the village of Stargazer.

He could even see the domed roof of the observatory peeking over the slope of the peach orchard and the rhododendron hedge that formed the boundary between the Martins' farm and Dr. Bhimani's lab and observatory.

That lab was the only Earth home Riggs and his brothers had known until Drago's mate, Arden, broke them out and brought them here.

They were still so close to the lab. And yet their lives were very different now.

At the lab, Riggs had lived a passive life. It was not unpleasant, except that his body and mind had craved work, even though he hadn't known it then.

And of course his mate had not been there.

The thought of Sage sent a shiver of desire down his spine, even as he despaired inwardly.

His intended was wise, hard-working, sensible, and a wild beauty with her full hips and flowing chestnut hair. Her every look made him crazy with the need to hold her and claim her. Every part of his heart, body and mind told him clearly that this woman was his destiny.

And he could see the blush in her cheeks when he came near. She felt it too. He was sure of it.

But she paid no mind to it at all.

He had watched her shiver with desire at his accidental touch, and then turn her head away and set the table as if nothing had happened.

Riggs was convinced she had an iron will. Her incredible

discipline would serve them well, especially once they had young to raise.

But for now it was making him crazy.

If only he had his brothers' gift for endless talking. Then maybe he could convince her that she should be his.

As things were, he had barely been able to speak two words to her.

He had not even told her that he had chosen her as his mate.

Though he had a feeling she wouldn't want to hear it.

Sage was a good enough talker for both of them. He spent his days working by her side and listening to a flow of her opinions on the farm, the way it was run now, and the way her grandmother had run it. Riggs knew exactly how she felt about politics, the new traffic in the village, the weather, the crops, and even her younger sister, Tansy, who frustrated her and inspired her fiercest love in nearly equal measures.

A woman who narrated her feelings so blithely was the perfect mate for a man who craved company but preferred to speak with his actions. Riggs sometimes felt that Sage sensed this and filled their silences in part to help him understand his new world, and in part to please him.

Or maybe she was just talking to prevent him from saying what they both knew he needed to say.

He spotted movement outside the farmhouse out of the corner of his eye, bringing him out of his reverie.

He turned to see Sage herself, looking out over the farm with a mug of coffee in her hands. Her long hair was still wet from the shower and she wore a pink t-shirt and a pair of cut-off blue jeans. Her expression was pleased - she was doing the same thing he was, enjoying the lay of the land as the dawn slowly illuminated the farm.

She glanced in his direction and he decided to go to her.

Before he could begin his descent, something dashed across the roof of the barn in his direction.

Without thinking, Riggs stepped backward.

The whole ladder tipped and he felt it going down before he could do anything to stop it.

He had just enough time to glimpse a squirrel that seemed almost as startled as he was, then the side of the barn flashed past his eyes and he was looking through the ladder at the sky as he plummeted to the ground.

He could hear Sage's scream and he was thankful she would not be able to see it when he made impact.

He landed hard on his back and the ladder bounced twice on his chest. As quickly as he could, he slipped out from under it and arranged his limbs naturally.

He was unhurt and felt no pain at all. This was his gift. He was virtually unbreakable.

But Dr. Bhimani had forbidden him from telling anyone about it, except for his true mate once they were bonded. And he had not staked his claim on Sage yet.

She tore down the lawn so fast he could feel the impact of her steps in the ground as she approached.

"Riggs," she gasped, dropping to her knees at his side.

"I'm okay," he said softly.

She smelled heavenly, like soap and fresh coffee, and the lighter muskier scent that was Sage herself.

"You aren't okay," she half-moaned. "You just fell from a thirty foot ladder. You're in shock."

"I wasn't all the way up," he said, hating himself for the lie. "I was coming down."

"You were coming down, alright," Sage said. "Right on your head."

He shifted, meaning to sit up and show her he wasn't

hurt.

"*Don't try to move*," she said firmly.

He paused automatically at the authority in her voice.

But then he went ahead and sat up anyway - he couldn't risk her wanting to call in a doctor.

"See," he said. "I'm fine."

She observed him, speechless for once.

Riggs was filled with a desire to fill the silence, but he had no idea what he was supposed to say. Then it came to him. Now was his chance.

"Sage," he said, emotion welling in his chest. "You are the smartest, most resourceful woman to inhabit the universe. In your wisdom, you already know my feelings, but I wish to speak them aloud to you. I adore you, Sage Martin. I choose you as my mate, the only woman I will ever bond with. Will you accept me?"

She gaped at him for a moment.

"You did hit your head," she said, recovering at last. "Wow, you are going to laugh later when I tell you what you just said. Let me find your brothers and see if they can help me get you back to the house. I know you won't want to go to the hospital, but maybe Dr. Bhimani can send over a nurse to check on you."

"Sage," Riggs said. He placed a hand on her arm and watched her pupils dilate as the pleasure rushed through her at his touch, just as it rushed through him. "I did not hit my head, and I don't need a nurse. I only need you. You do not have to answer me now. I just wanted you to know what's in my heart."

He hopped to his feet and offered her his hand.

She took it, an expression of wonder on her face.

He hoped it had more to do with his words than his apparent skill at falling.

3

SAGE

S age looked up at Riggs, amazed.

He studied her with an expression of concern, which only made his already angelic face more handsome.

She closed her hand around his and allowed him to help her up.

When she was standing, she realized how close she was to him - his big body inches from hers, her hand still lost in his.

The air between them seemed to sizzle. She felt her body start to respond the way it always did when he was near - a planet orbiting a sun.

Her dreams had taught her well. She could practically feel him kissing her already.

"What are your plans for the day?" he asked her.

It took her a moment to make sense of the words.

When she put them together she felt the blood rushing to her cheeks. She was in an agony of attraction and he was asking for her daily agenda. He had meant what he said about not needing an answer to his outrageous proposal right away.

She chided herself for the unexpected wave of disappointment that washed over her.

"I was planning to go to the printers in town after breakfast," she said. "I need to have flyers made."

"Someone in town makes aviation devices?" Riggs lifted his eyebrows, impressed. "Where do you need to fly?"

"What? Oh. No," she said. "I see why you thought that, but no. Flyers are just advertisements printed on a sheet of paper."

"I see," he nodded. But he didn't look convinced.

"Here," she said, letting go of his hand to slide her cell phone out of her pocket. "Here's the one I'm having made today. I'll go back after lunch to pick them up and see if I can get some of the local businesses to hang them in their windows."

She handed him the phone.

He looked down at it and chuckled.

"Do you get it?" she asked. She hadn't though he would understand the joke.

"This is an idiom, right?" he asked, handing the phone back to her.

"Yes," she smiled.

The top of the flyer said, *Take your sweetie to Martin's Bounty for Pick-Your-Own-Peaches.*

The image below showed a cartoon couple under two peach trees. In a dialogue balloon, one character said to the other, "You're a peach!"

Below the picture it said, *Here at Martin's Bounty the skies are blue, the berries are ripe and everything is peachy keen!*

"This is a very good advertisement," Riggs said. "It makes me want to pick peaches."

"Thanks," Sage said, unable to hide her grin.

She enjoyed working on things like the flyer and designing the signs for the peach pick. Although she had an accounting background, she'd always had a fondness for marketing and graphic design.

"May I accompany you to town?" Riggs asked.

"This morning?" Sage asked.

"And this afternoon," he offered.

Sage was a little surprised. Riggs and his brothers normally fed and mucked up after the animals in the afternoons and then took a swim in the pond. They clearly enjoyed the time together with the animals, and swimming was a favorite pastime of everyone on the farm.

"Are you sure?" she asked, not wanting to cut in on his time with his brothers, she could only imagine how much they must rely on each other to make sense of this strange world. "It will be a lot of walking around in town and talking to people to get permission to post the flyers."

Riggs was not just the quiet type. The big alien was deeply, profoundly silent. She really couldn't imagine him approaching strangers to ask if he could hang flyers in their windows.

"Sounds good," he said, giving her a nod.

She was surprised at how delighted she felt, as if she were headed to a birthday party this morning instead of a dreaded task.

"Morning guys," Arden said from the barn door.

Drago was with her, their hands intertwined. The two of them looked, supremely, wildly happy.

"Good morning," Sage replied. "You're up early."

"We'll help you with breakfast," Drago offered.

"No need," Sage told him. "It's already taken care of."

"Otis?" Arden asked.

Sage nodded.

"I guess it's cake for breakfast," Arden laughed.

"Oh, we know that one," Drago said. "*Dad is great. Give us the chocolate cake!*"

"You have *so* much catching up to do when it comes to pop culture," Arden said playfully.

The two of them headed up the hill toward the picnic table, where Otis was setting out the morning's treats.

Sage turned to Riggs.

He smiled at her, blue eyes crinkling.

"What are you smiling about?" she asked, smiling back.

He shrugged and jogged up the hill to join her.

4

SAGE

Maybe it was just the sugar rush from the almond mini croissants, but Sage was feeling fantastic as she pulled out of the gravel lot in Grandma Helen's pick-up truck.

The morning was clear and pleasant, still cool after last night's showers.

Riggs sat by her side. His big body barely fit in the cab and his thighs, encased in skintight jeans, were so close to hers she could practically feel the heat pouring off him.

He looked out the window, a pleased expression on his handsome face.

"It really is nice out," Sage agreed with his unspoken thought. "It will probably heat up this afternoon though. Hopefully we can be the first one at the printers' and pick up early too."

"Mmm," Riggs agreed.

"You know, I can't believe that Grandma Helen did all this herself every year," Sage marveled, not for the first time. "I mean she had a few hired hands, but all the cooking, organizing the tourist picks, keeping the books, she did it all herself."

"Was it difficult for her?" Riggs asked.

Sage thought about that as they passed the last of the farmland and neared the little village.

"I'm sure it wasn't easy," she said. "There were bad years. And even in a good year, there's so much work to be done. But she always seemed happy. Do you know what I mean?"

Riggs nodded thoughtfully.

"I mean there's a certain kind of person who is busy and they talk it to death," Sage said. "*I'm so busy, I'm so stressed.* That wasn't her at all. And there's the kind of person who wears thin under stress. They might be suffering in silence but you can see the exhaustion in their eyes. But Grandma Helen enjoyed hard work, so I think it was difficult, but that kept it interesting for her."

She smiled, thinking of Grandma Helen at the end of a long day on the farm, sitting in her rocker out on the porch, telling little Sage and Tansy funny stories about the chickens or the farm hands or her own blunders.

"Do you miss her?" Riggs asked.

Sage's breath caught in her throat.

Of all things, she had not expected that question. But his instinct was right. It was just like Riggs to listen so well that he could get to the heart of the matter.

"I do," she said, nodding.

Riggs nodded too.

"I guess I've been so busy worrying about Tansy's mourning I never really thought about my own," Sage said after a moment.

"You're like her," Riggs said.

"Like Tansy?" Sage asked.

"Like your grandmother," Riggs said softly. "You work hard to care for your sister and for the rest of us."

Warmth bloomed in Sage's chest. It was a wonderful compliment. The more so because she was surprised by it, yet knew it was true.

"Grandma Helen was a good example for us," Sage allowed.

They had arrived in the little town. She pulled into a space right across from the post office.

"Here we are," she said.

Riggs hopped out and opened the door for her before she even had her purse out of the console.

"Thank you." She rewarded his chivalry with a smile, which he returned.

It was still quiet in town. The coffee shop on the corner was bustling, but almost nothing else was open.

"It's this one," she told Riggs, indicating the copy shop.

Since the arrival of the aliens in Stargazer, the little town had re-embraced the outer space theme they'd taken on decades ago, when they first expected extraterrestrial contact.

The print shop's formerly faded sign had been replaced by a purple awning with *Cosmic Copies* emblazoned on it in gold lettering.

She pushed open the door, setting the sleigh bells hung over it jingling.

"Someone's up early," Howard crowed from behind the counter.

"Hey, Howard," Sage called to him.

Howard Gillespie had been working at Cosmic Copies since Sage was a little girl. And he was an old man with a white beard back then.

"Hey yourself, Sage Martin," Howard chuckled. "Oh, who's your friend there? Paul Bunyan? *Ha*."

She gave him a moment to laugh at his own joke.

"I am Riggs. I work on the Martins' farm," Riggs explained politely.

"I'll bet you do, son," Howard said. "You look like you could work the whole farm all by yourself."

Sage worried that Riggs would not understand the joke.

But the big alien wisely kept his trap shut, studying the elderly printer carefully, as if he might contain important clues.

"I'd love to get flyers made," Sage said.

"Oh, right," Howard ripped his eyes away from Riggs. "Same Peach-Pickin' flyers on orange stock, like your grandma always ordered. Not a problem."

He didn't even look up from his computer.

For a moment, Sage thought about just going with what Helen had always done.

"Sage has designed a new flyer," Riggs said.

Howard looked up at her over his bifocals in surprise.

"You did, eh?" he asked. "Let's have a look."

"I can email it to you," Sage offered as she pulled it up on her phone.

Howard pointed to his email address on his business card on the counter.

She tapped it into her phone and hit send, then waited for him to open it.

"Well now, let's see," Howard said, bending over the computer screen and scowling at it, as if he were trying to figure out alien technology rather than just opening the email program he used each day to do business.

At last he succeeded.

"*Peachy keen,*" Howard said from behind the counter. "That's cute, Sage. It's simple and funny - really nice work."

"Thanks," she said with a sincere smile.

Although she knew her accounting talents were wasted designing flyers for a tourist farm, Sage enjoyed the praise.

Once the farm was up and running in the black, there would be no place for her. Tansy and Burton could hire some hands. Arden and Drago would most likely stick around too.

And Sage would get back to her entry level accountant position at Myriax Pharmaceuticals. She'd already burned through a lot of the unpaid time off she could legally take on the Family Medical Leave Act.

She found herself considering how Riggs might fare in the real world.

She watched him looking around the print shop. He spun to take in the brightly colored sheaves of paper, the tiny boxes of paperclips and pencil erasers. She wondered what he made of it all.

Though all three men had adapted to farm life quickly and knew the place inside out, it was moments like this one when she realized how unrealistic it was to expect that they could easily join the regular world.

She and the other women had experienced a lifetime of preparation in language, culture and manners beginning when they were incredibly impressionable, and too small to walk or talk.

As she watched, he fingered a pyramid of unsharpened pencils.

The lowest one slipped out and pencils rained down on the floor.

"My apologies," Riggs muttered, bending to retrieve the pencils. "I thought it was solid.

"No worries, son," Howard said. "Just stick 'em in the bin. I just stack them up for fun."

"Thanks," Sage said, leaning over the counter again.

"The pretty ones are never the sharpest," Howard whispered and then gave her a garish wink. "Fifty copies on white card stock okay?"

"Uh, yes, thank you," she said, trying not to be offended on Riggs's behalf. "We'll be back after lunch."

Howard nodded. "Anytime after eleven is fine."

She turned to see Riggs had re-stacked the pencils in a pyramid shape already.

"That was quick," she said. "Ready to go?"

Riggs winked at her - a nice friendly wink, very much unlike the one Howard had just given her - and nodded.

5

RIGGS

R iggs observed his intended as she drove the vehicle back to the farm.

Sage gazed at the road before her with her usual determined expression, both hands firmly on the steering wheel.

Burton had described riding in the truck with Tansy as being similar to taking a ship out of Ajyxdrive. But Sage was slow and steady at the wheel, which Riggs appreciated very much.

There was so much he appreciated about her.

Her hair had dried in the sun. It fell around her shoulders, looking as glossy soft as a kitten. Her full breasts bounced and shivered at each bump in the road.

Riggs knew it was the height of bad manners to stare, but he was having a hard time helping himself. His body was beginning to make demands that could not be fulfilled until she accepted him.

He forced himself to look away, wishing more than anything that Sage would speak. Her thoughts and feelings were even more attractive to him than her body. But they did not have the same unintended physical consequences for him.

Usually.

"I wonder if any of the newcomers will be interested in picking peaches," Sage pondered out loud, as if in answer to his unspoken request.

Riggs had a hard time understanding how anyone could fail to be interested in picking peaches. But this was something the women in his life worried about very much.

"I guess they only want to see aliens," Sage went on. "Though isn't it funny? They would be much more likely to see aliens on our farm than they are in the open air market in town."

She laughed and Riggs laughed with her.

"At any rate, we only need to hit the crowds we got last year," Sage went on. "Since the Wilsons aren't open for tourists maybe we'll get a few extra customers. Though that means the Wilsons won't be advertising either. I always thought Bud got people in the mood for pick-your-own when he drove his truck around with the logo on the side. Well, here we are."

Riggs was startled to find that they were home already.

They pulled up the gravel drive and Sage gasped.

Riggs followed her gaze to the source of her alarm.

"I guess someone spotted that ladder and decided to play a prank," Sage said, a mix of anger and surprise in her voice.

In his haste to get to breakfast, he must have left the ladder out.

The big sign over the barn no longer read *Welcome to Martin's Bounty*. Bright red spray paint adjusted the lettering so that it now said:

WELCOME *to Martian's Booty*

"DO THEY KNOW WE'RE HERE?" Riggs asked.

"No," Sage said immediately. "At least I don't think so. I hope not."

A line formed on her forehead. She was concerned too.

"But it's not good that they're referencing aliens," she said.

"We are not from Mars," he reminded her.

"No, but to a bigoted vandal it's all the same thing," she said. "Plus there's the other part."

"Ah, yes, the part about the treasure," he said. "What do they mean by that? Are they pirates of some sort?"

"Oh," Sage said. "That's not what booty means in this context. They mean the, er, other booty."

"What other booty?" Riggs searched his memory for some other use of the term. "Like a baby shoe?"

"Oh dear," said Sage. "Booty can also refer to a woman's... buttocks."

"But there are only male aliens on this farm," Riggs pointed out, feeling more confused by the moment.

"It implies, um, mating," Sage said. "So if they are calling this farm Martian's Booty, they're saying that this is where women who have sex with aliens live." Her face was red as a beet by the time she was finished.

Riggs looked at the sign again, this time admiring how efficiently the sign painter had adapted those two short words into a remarkably apt description.

But he could also sense that it would not please Sage for him to say so.

Besides, mating was private, and this sign was public,

and therefore dreadful manners, no matter how truthful it was.

"This is an affront to your sister's honor," he realized out loud.

"Oh god, we can't let Tansy see it," Sage said.

"She will be offended," Riggs agreed.

"No," Sage said. "She will probably think it's funny. But then she'll start to worry about someone vandalizing the farm."

"Do you think she should be worried?" Riggs asked.

"I think this is the work of teenagers," Sage said. "It seems like a one-time thing. And it was my fault for not making sure the ladder was put away."

"I was the one who was using the ladder," Riggs said. "But I'll run up and take the sign down. We can repaint it and no one will have to see this."

"Who would do this?" Sage wondered out loud. "Most of the teenagers are at the pool all day."

It occurred to Riggs that the only person on the farm who wasn't usually there was Otis.

"I'll just climb up and take it down," he said, choosing not to upset Sage with this idea. Surely Otis was sincerely sorry for what he had done before. Besides, Riggs couldn't understand how the man could bake their breakfast all morning and then vandalize their sign the moment they left.

It just didn't make sense.

6

RIGGS

R iggs could hear his brothers' laughter on the hill behind the barn.

While he had removed the offending sign, hidden it, and properly stored the ladder, Sage had headed inside to prepare lunch.

Riggs decided to head up the hillside and see what was so amusing.

At breakfast, Arden had assigned his brothers the task of cleaning up the empty bushel baskets for the tourists. He could see that they had a stack of baskets lined up and a hose at the ready.

Drago was in charge of the water and Burton was moving the baskets to be hosed off individually.

But each time Burton carefully placed a basket on the tarp and turned around to retrieve the next one, Drago squirted him with the hose.

Both men were laughing their heads off and Riggs could see that the basket washing wasn't going very quickly. But he was very glad to see them.

"Hello, brother," Drago called to him. "May I squirt you with the hose in a playful manner?"

Before Riggs could answer, Drago aimed the nozzle at him and sprayed.

The cool water felt fantastic on a hot day, but Riggs pretended to be angry and charged his brother like a rhinoceros.

Drago yelped and dropped the hose.

Burton promptly picked it up and waved it around wildly as Riggs lifted his brother off his feet and slammed him to the ground.

Riggs was feeling victorious when one of the peach trees seemed to reach out a root to trip him as he turned around.

"No fair, you used your gift," he spluttered, not mentioning that thanks to his own gift, he was completely unhurt.

Drago just laughed like a wild hyena.

Burton sprayed Drago down, calming him considerably.

Then he turned the hose on Riggs.

"Okay, okay," Riggs laughed, standing and lifting his hands in surrender. "We give up, Burton."

Burton smiled and sprayed himself with the hose.

"Did you have fun with Sage?" Drago asked, waggling his eyebrows as he got to his feet.

"Yes, but not in the way you are implying," Riggs replied.

"I'm not implying anything," Drago said, feigning innocence.

"Well, your eyebrows are," Riggs retorted.

Burton laughed and then Riggs laughed too.

Drago waggled his eyebrows again and clapped Riggs on the shoulder.

"Really, brother, how are things with Sage?" he asked.

"I'm not sure," Riggs said. "They're going slowly. But she's my mate. I told her this morning that I chose her."

Burton nodded, looking impressed.

"You hadn't told her yet?" Drago exclaimed, smacking him on the shoulder again, this time as if to scold him.

"No," Riggs said, fighting the urge to shove back. "Sage is not like your mates. She is thoughtful. It will take time for her to accept this idea."

"Tansy is thoughtful," Burton retorted.

"I did not mean polite, I meant… ponderous," Riggs explained. "Sage doesn't make decisions lightly. But I have faith that she will accept me."

"She will, brother," Drago said lightly. "And then we will all be mated."

Riggs often wished he shared Drago's easy confidence. The world seemed to offer itself to his easygoing brother. Riggs had to be more patient.

"He's right," Burton said softly. "And so are you. Sage will need more time to think it over. She likes to have a plan. Soon you will be part of it."

The truth of this struck Riggs and he was deeply moved. He threw an arm around each of their shoulders.

"What would I do without you, my brothers?" he asked. "This world only seems to make sense when I have you to help me observe it."

"We are a team," Drago said firmly. "We all need each other."

Someone cleared her throat behind them. He didn't need to hear any words to know exactly who it was. Riggs spun around to confirm that it was indeed Sage standing behind them, and shot her a sheepish grin.

"I see you're having fun with this job," she said, eyes twinkling.

Riggs wondered helplessly how long she'd been standing there.

"I just came up to let you know that lunch will be ready in about ten minutes, so come on down when you finish up," she said.

"We will, Sage," Riggs told her.

She smiled and then turned and headed back down the hillside.

7

SAGE

S age willed herself to walk carefully down the hillside back to the kitchen. She would not cry over what she had overheard.

What would I do without you, my brothers?

Riggs's rhetorical question stung.

Sage couldn't believe that just an hour ago she had been asking herself whether he could come with her and assimilate to the outside world. She'd been worried about how he would get used to grocery shopping and elevators.

It had never occurred to her to wonder if he would miss his brothers, or if he would even be willing to go anywhere without them.

They were his only connection to his past life. And the more Sage thought about it, the more it made sense. Of course they helped each other to adjust to this new life. Of course they needed each other.

Even Dr. Bhimani had not sent just one alien to the farm. She had sent three.

They looked like men, and they had a man's needs. But their short time on this planet also made them like children.

Sage could not imagine Tansy being taken from her when they were small. It would have been unthinkable not to have a sister with whom she could untangle the mysteries of the world.

Sage had nearly reached the farm house now. The roses climbing up the back trellis were in full bloom. They trailed up the side of the house, their flaming orange color trumpeting the return of summer. But their glory was in full contrast to the gloom in Sage's heart.

She could not take Riggs with her. She would not separate him from his brothers. And the farm was not the place for her.

"Sage," Otis called out. "I'm so glad you're here."

She had left him alone in the kitchen for five minutes. His only job was to flip the grilled cheese sandwiches when they were cooked on the first side.

But she stepped into the kitchen to the scent of burning bread.

Otis stood in front of the griddle, one of Grandma Helen's aprons barely covering his chest, a spatula in one hand, his other hand fanning a newspaper to dissipate the smoke.

"Oh dear," Sage said, marching into the fray.

She bumped him aside with her hips, grabbed another spatula from the can on the counter and started flipping the sandwiches. One was already on the floor in front of the stove.

"That'll be mine," Otis said quickly. "Ten second rule."

"I think it's a five second rule," Sage said. "And there's no scientific basis for it. Whatever it landed on would have already contaminated it."

Otis picked up the sandwich anyway and put it on a plate.

Sage couldn't help but notice that one side wasn't toasted at all.

"Give it to me," she sighed.

He handed it over and she dumped it on the griddle. Maybe she could cook the germs off it.

The other sandwiches took some prying but she managed to flip them.

"How's the soup coming along?" she asked.

Otis blinked at her.

"There's tomato soup on the counter, the can opener's in the drawer," she said, pointing at the soup.

"Sorry. I guess I'm really more of a baker," Otis explained as he grabbed the can opener. "The bread for the sandwiches is fresh. I baked it this morning."

"That's impressive," Sage allowed, looking at the bread in the pan. It did smell delicious. "And don't worry too much about it."

"I'm sure I'll get better at other kinds of cooking if I spend more time here," Otis said.

Sage was surprised that he was planning to spend much more time with them. Surely he would feel he had paid off his debt after a few days.

She looked over at him and he smiled at her sheepishly. Somehow it didn't seem as endearing as when Riggs did it.

She caught a glimpse of something bright red on his hands.

He grabbed a towel right away and tried to cover them, but it was too late, she had seen.

It hit her that Otis might have some other reason to be here at the farm. He might still be planning to sabotage them.

And he had started with vandalizing the sign on the barn.

"What's on your hands?" she asked.

"Oh, er, uh," he stammered, further entangling his hands in the towel.

"I already saw, you don't need to hide them," Sage said sternly.

"It was supposed to be a surprise," he said miserably.

"Some surprise," Sage said. "How could you?"

"I know, I know, you said we all need protein, but I couldn't help it," he told her. "Everyone loves red velvet cake."

"What?" Sage asked.

Otis opened the refrigerator and pointed inside.

Sage stepped over and saw a two tiered, lavishly frosted cake.

"I was going to surprise everyone after dinner, but you, uh, caught me red-handed," Otis said with a nervous laugh. "I had a little mishap with the food coloring."

"Oh, wow," Sage said, feeling terrible for suspecting him. It seemed pretty far-fetched that he might have vandalized their sign, then run back inside and baked an entire cake as an alibi.

"I made it while you were in town this morning," he said proudly. "Still can't believe I got it done before you walked in the door."

"Is something burning?" Tansy asked as she strode in the back door.

"Shoot," Sage said, dashing back to the stove to get the sandwiches off the griddle.

8

RIGGS

A fter lunch, Riggs sat beside Sage in the truck once again.

This time she was strangely quiet. The relaxed smile she wore this morning had been replaced with a look of concern.

It occurred to him that she must be worrying about the vandal.

"Do not worry about the sign," he told her. "I put it in the back of the truck when no one was watching. I hope we can purchase paint in town and fix it before we go back to the farm."

This made her smile. She flashed him a grateful look that filled his chest with warmth.

"Tansy will never see it," he told her solemnly. "Also, I had a thought about who might have done this."

"Really?" Sage asked. "I had an idea too, but I was wrong."

"I do not like to make an accusation without proof, but Otis was trying to harm your operations just a few days ago.

Now he is at the farm early each morning," Riggs said carefully. "Do you think he would do this?"

"I thought the same thing," Sage nodded thoughtfully. "But he has a pretty good alibi."

"What was he doing?" Riggs asked. "I thought everyone else was working while we were gone."

"They were, but so was he," Sage said. "He made a two-layer red velvet cake while we were out. He didn't have time to vandalize the sign. I've seen enough *Great British Baking Show* to know what's possible. There's no way he could have done both in the time we were gone. Besides, if he really wanted to harm our business, he could have just kept his mouth shut about the bees."

Riggs was not familiar with the show she referred to, but Sage sounded convinced.

He was both disappointed and relieved. Of course he would not want to think that anyone they trusted would betray them.

But it rattled his senses to think that someone who intended harm to Sage and her family had slipped past him somehow. Every fiber of his being demanded that he keep her safe.

"Here we are," Sage said.

They pulled into a parking space close to Cosmic Copies and went inside, sending the bells on the door jingling.

"Hey there," Howard said. "Your flyers are right here."

"Great," Sage replied, hurrying to the counter.

Riggs looked around, wondering if the store had painting supplies.

The bright interior of the little store was so cheerful he felt like he was inside one of Tansy and Sage's old children's books that were still kept on a shelf by the fireplace.

A riot of colorful sheaves of paper lined one wall of the

shop. Carousels of books and cards lined another. And in between were bins of writing implements and dozens of shelves of items he couldn't even identify.

"What are you looking for?" Sage asked when she was finished with their purchase.

"I was wondering if they had painting things here," Riggs told her.

"Good thinking," Sage said, rewarding him with a gentle smile. "The hardware store would probably have better paint for an outdoor sign. We'll go there last so we won't have to carry the paint supplies on our walk."

Riggs smiled back at her and nodded.

She walked toward the door and he scrambled to reach it first so he could open it for her.

"Thank you, Riggs," she said, brushing past him and leaving a trail of her intoxicating scent in her wake.

The jingle of the bells echoed the song in Riggs's heart and it was all he could do not to wrap his arms around her and kiss her.

Soon, he told himself. *Soon.*

9

SAGE

S age stepped onto the sidewalk and Riggs followed.

The milder weather meant the citizens of Stargazer were out in full force. Cafe tables had been set up along the tree-lined sidewalks and people with bright canvas shopping bags wandered in and out of the stores.

A contingent of tourists in souvenir t-shirts wandered around, stopping for selfies against the backdrop of all the space-inspired shop names.

Sage wondered how Riggs would react to all this. He was so reserved and quiet. It was probably the wrong day to ask him to follow her around while she asked to post flyers.

But this was prime peach picking season and the farm opened for tourists in a less than a week. It was now or never.

She snuck a glance over at her tall, dark and handsome companion.

He observed the street with interest, his gaze taking in the tables, the people, the bright colors.

"It's a busy day for Stargazer," Sage observed.

"Everyone seems happy," Riggs said.

He was right, she hadn't noticed, but there was a holiday feel in town today. It was likely the weather, making everyone lighthearted.

"So where do we hang the flyers?" Riggs asked.

"Let's start at the post office," Sage said.

They crossed Jupiter Avenue and headed down Pluto Place to the post office - one of the few buildings in town that hadn't adopted the space motif. She supposed that was to be expected for a branch of the federal government. She also knew they stocked more space themed postage stamps and postcards than she had ever seen in one place, so it wasn't like they weren't doing their part.

If the usual counter clerk was on duty this would be a baptism by fire for Riggs. At least she would have a better idea of how he interacted with other people.

They crossed the small town square and passed the bird-poop speckled clock tower and the modern art installation. When they got to the door, Riggs opened it for her.

As soon as the blast of conditioned air and tinny John Phillip Sousa music hit her, Sage knew she was in luck. The other postal workers listened to jazz on the radio during their shifts.

"Oh my heavens, Sage Martin is that you?" an excited voice demanded before Sage was entirely sure she could have been spotted, let alone identified.

"Hello, Lainey," she said.

The small blonde woman behind the counter clasped her hands together joyfully.

"I'm so glad to see you, Sage, honey," she said. "I was very sorry about your grandmother. We miss her a lot."

"Thank you," Sage said, surprised at the lump forming in her throat.

"I noticed you and your sister are getting mail at the

farm," Lainey said, eyes sparkling. "Does this mean you're taking over?"

"We're taking it one day at a time," Sage said.

"And who's this?" Lainey asked, looking up at Riggs as if she had just noticed him, and liked what she saw.

"I'm Riggs," he said, stepping forward before Sage had a chance to introduce him. "We're bringing around flyers to let everyone know about Pick-Your-Own-Peaches at Martin's Bounty. May we hang one here?"

Sage almost fell over. She had never known Riggs to be so quick to speak.

"Well, this is a government facility, so I can't just hang it in the window," Lainey said. "But we do have a community bulletin board in the town green. I'll get the key for you so you can hang it up."

"Thank you," Riggs replied. "That would be great."

They watched as Lainey reached for the key hanging on the wall beside the counter. Her short stature made retrieving it a challenge. She stretched up and gave a little hop and missed it by an inch.

"Let me help you," Riggs offered.

"What a gentleman," Lainey said with a big smile, opening the door to let him behind the counter.

He plucked it off the wall while Lainey looked up at him, examining him as carefully as if she expected to take a quiz on his exact physical specifications as soon as he was finished.

When he turned to her, she shooed him back out the door.

"There you go, just bring it back after you put up your flyer," she said, winking at Sage.

"Thank you, we'll be right back with it," Sage said.

Riggs held the door for her and they ventured back into

the sunshine on the way to the bulletin board.

He handed her the key and she used it to open the glass door.

When they had hung the flyer between a handwritten ad for a local karate studio, and an official notice of thanks to the town for sending the scouts to their annual canoe trip to Heaven Falls, Sage locked the glass again.

"I'll bring it back in," Riggs offered, jogging toward the post office entrance with the key.

Sage stared after him, amazed at this confident man with whom she was spending her afternoon.

It turned out his easy way with Lainey wasn't a fluke.

A few hours later, the box of flyers was nearly empty.

They had visited most of the storefronts in town. Riggs had even gone into the tattoo parlor and made a new friend. The whole town was lined with Pick-Your-Own-Peaches info. At least if things didn't go well this weekend it wouldn't be because no one knew about the farm being open.

"Shall we head over to the hardware store and then go home?" Sage asked.

"That sounds good," Riggs agreed.

They entered the door under the *Helios Hardware* sign.

"What can I help you with?" the clerk asked. "Oh, hey, Sage."

"Hi, Angel, what's new?" Sage asked.

"Not much, wow—" Angel replied, cutting herself off when she got a load of Riggs.

"Hi there," Riggs said politely. "I'm Riggs."

Sage got plenty of fresh air and exercise and a shower every morning. She knew she was young and healthy and she had always taken a bit of pride in her wavy brown hair.

But Angel Hicks sported a more cultivated look that included plenty of lip gloss and a lacy, low cut tank top. Sage could hardly blame the woman for playing up her femininity since she worked in a male-dominated industry. But as Riggs approached Angel with his hand extended, Sage couldn't help worrying he might find her... interesting.

If he did, he didn't show it.

As Angel gazed up at him, wide-eyed, Riggs shook her hand politely and stepped back, his eyes never going south of her neck.

"Angel Hicks," Angel breathed, a moment too late.

"We would like to buy some paint, Angel Hicks," Riggs said. "Do you have good paint for an outdoor sign?"

The mention of a need for something in the range of Angel's expertise snapped her out of her trance, and she launched herself out from behind the counter and marched down one of the dusty aisles.

"I sure do," she said. "Follow me."

Sage and Riggs trailed after her and found themselves looking at a row of paint cans and canisters of spray paint.

"Enamel is the best for outdoor use, though acrylic is less expensive," Angel explained. "Personally, I like to finish an exterior sign with a wood sealant to really protect the paint."

"We'll go with whatever you suggest," Sage said. "We want a white background and we'll do black lettering."

Angel nodded as if they were soldiers at war, and Sage was her superior, about to send her on a mission behind enemy lines.

While Angel applied herself to snagging various cans and brushes off the shelves, Sage watched Riggs examine the shelves.

"What are you looking at?" she asked.

"Have a lot of people been buying sign paint lately?" he asked, his hand skimming a canister of red spray paint.

"Sure," Angel said, emerging from the shelves. "Lots of local folks like to touch up their signs from year to year. Or change them up. Especially with all the newcomers around lately."

"Anyone buy red paint?" Riggs asked.

"I guess," Angel replied. "People buy all sorts of colors."

Riggs nodded, looking a little disappointed.

But Sage was thunderstruck.

Riggs might be on the quiet side, and at times his inexperience on this planet could make him seem childlike, but the big alien was anything but innocent.

He was attractive, yes, but that was not his most remarkable quality. He was smart, charismatic, and he had a drive so singular that it felt familiar.

It felt like her own.

They paid for their purchases quickly and then emerged into the sunshine once again.

Riggs turned to her and she nearly lost herself in his startlingly azure eyes.

"Where should we go to paint the sign?" he asked.

His voice was husky, as if he were noticing her in the same way. As if he wanted to be alone with her.

She found herself naming the one place she knew she shouldn't mention. The place she had often escaped to during the summers she'd spent on the farm with her grandparents.

A place where they would most definitely be alone.

RIGGS

R iggs looked around the clearing.

Sage had parked the truck half a mile away and they had carried the sign and supplies through what felt like the wilderness for fifteen silent minutes.

"Where are we?" he asked, looking around at the circle of small shelters surrounding a shady area with a stone pit at its center.

"This is a scouts' campground," Sage explained. "But the kids are at Heaven Falls for their annual canoe trip. We have the place to ourselves."

Riggs noticed the color staining her cheeks a moment after the words left her mouth.

He tried not to smile, though he felt a sense of victory that she wanted to be alone with him, even if it was only to paint a sign.

"Is there a good place to work?" he asked.

"The mess hall," she replied, heading toward one of the rustic looking shelters.

When they got closer, he could see that the walls were

made of screens. Two rows of picnic tables filled the single room in the structure. Sage opened the door and flicked a switch. A ceiling fan turned on but no light.

"I guess the bulb is out." She shrugged. "It's still light enough in here to work."

She placed the sign on one of the tables and Riggs unpacked the cans of paint and sealant, and the brushes from the bag he carried.

"What are these for?" he asked, pulling two wooden sticks and a metal loop out of the bag.

"The key is to open the paint cans and the sticks are to stir the paint," Sage told him.

"What about these?" he asked, pulling out a copy of the Stargazer Gazette and three bottles of water.

"The newspaper will protect the table from being damaged by the paint," Sage said. "One water is to clean the sign before we paint it."

"And the other two?"

"Those are for us," she said. "That was a long walk."

Riggs laughed and watched as she spread the newspaper on the table.

"Want me to clean the sign?" he offered.

"Sure," she said.

He took the sign and one of the water bottles outside and did his best to get it clean.

When he returned to the mess hall, Sage had already opened one of the paint cans and was stirring it. The paint was creamy and white - watching Sage's delicate hand swirl the stick around in it was almost hypnotic.

"Okay, I think it's ready," she announced.

Riggs found the largest brush.

"That's perfect for the white background," Sage said approvingly. "Do you want to do it?"

"Sure," he said. He was pleased, he'd been curious about the consistency of the white liquid.

Sage gestured for him to begin.

He dipped the brush gently into the paint and applied some to the wooden sign. It was satisfying to feel it go on smoothly and to see it covering the offensive words.

"Paint with the grain of the wood," Sage suggested, moving her own hand left to right to show him.

He tried again and noticed how easily the brush moved along the surface of the sign.

It was silent in the room except for the calls of the birds outside. The air swirled cool against his skin in the wake of the fan.

And Sage stood so close beside him, her presence not engaging any of the five senses he had learned about, but stimulating him in a different way, until his body thrummed like a tightly strung violin.

The moment seemed to stretch for hours as she watched him smooth away the writing on the sign until it was a wash of snowy white.

He placed the brush down on the newspaper and turned to her.

"You have a little paint, right there," she murmured, going up on her toes and extending her hand to his cheek.

He grasped her wrist in his hand before she could touch him, and pressed his lips to her palm.

She gasped but did not pull away. Instead, her arm relaxed in his hold, as if she were melting.

Sage gazed up at him, lips slightly parted, her big brown eyes telling him everything her voice would not.

The air between them sizzled and Riggs suddenly thought of Zeno's dichotomy paradox - two bodies halving the distance between themselves an infinite number of times, never touching.

He had to go all the way.

"Sage, may I kiss you?" he whispered.

She nodded.

He bent to press his lips to hers and it was everything he had dared to imagine and more. Her lips were so soft and sweet.

She went up on her toes again, sliding her arms around his neck, maddening him with the press of her breasts against his chest.

He wrapped his arms around her, pulling her closer, deepening their kiss.

Sage whimpered slightly against his mouth and he licked her lips, plunging his tongue inside when she parted them for him.

He had seen this in movies, read about it, but nothing prepared him for the actual intimacy of tasting her mouth, feeling her sweet tongue caress his.

Desire raged in his blood and he was torn by his own opposing needs - his body's fierce demand that he claim her immediately and his heart's instinct not to rush, not to miss any facet of this tremulous new experience.

And he would not make the mating bond before she had accepted him.

But he could feel Sage's nipples graze his chest through the thin fabric that separated them. Her heart was beating so fast. Her body pressed to him as if she wanted him to consume her.

He knew what she needed. He would give her every pleasure imaginable without claiming her, if she would allow it.

The idea excited him terribly and he kissed her with

renewed fervor, until he felt her nails sink into his shoulders.

As gently as he could, he lifted her in his arms.

She wrapped her legs around his waist without breaking their kiss.

He carried her to the closest table that wasn't covered in painting supplies, and sat her on it.

"Riggs," she murmured as he pulled away to look at her.

"You are my mate," he told her roughly. "But I cannot ask you to accept me now. Just let me please you."

She blinked up at him.

He pulled his t-shirt over his head and relished the way her eyes went wider as she stared at his chest. He was glad his body excited her. He had not earned the muscles, any more than she had earned her soft curves or dark eyes, but he was grateful if they gave each other pleasure.

He rolled up his shirt and placed it on the table behind her, a perfect pillow.

She looked up at him hungrily.

He kissed her again, gentleness forgotten for a moment as he slid his hands under the hem of her shirt and lifted it slowly.

She raised her arms, making it easy for him to remove it.

His heart pounded in his chest and he pulled back slightly to look at her again.

She was exquisite. Her skin was smooth and tan except for a dark freckle above her belly button, and her breasts were generous, nearly spilling over the lacy contraption that held them prisoner.

"Sage," he breathed.

She blushed pink but did not look away.

He took a deep breath.

This is literally what you were made for. No need to be nervous.

She held perfectly still as he wrapped his arms around her, found the tiny hooks and released them. He eased the straps from her shoulders, kissing the tiny indentations the garment had left there.

She tilted her head slightly, as if in invitation, and he nuzzled the place where her neck met her shoulder. She smelled like the orchard, peaches and cinnamon and summer.

Need bubbled up inside him and it took everything he had to restrain it.

For her. Be patient for her.

He pulled back slightly and was beside himself all over again at the sight of her bare breasts. Each pale orb was as beautiful as the moons of Aerie.

She arched her back slightly, as if to offer herself to him.

He reached out and stroked one rosy nipple lightly.

Sage gasped.

Worried that he had hurt her, he searched her eyes, but they were hazy with need.

He cupped her breast and lowered his face to taste it.

Her nipple stiffened further on his tongue.

He licked it into his mouth and Sage moaned and gripped his upper arms.

Overcome with lust he feasted on her breasts, first one and then the other, glorying in her every sigh and moan until her grip on his arms tightened and he knew it wasn't enough anymore. She needed more.

He cupped her cheek in his hand, kissing her forehead tenderly as he lowered her to rest her head on his t-shirt behind her.

She looked up at him with such trust in her eyes that it almost hurt his heart.

I love you. I will never leave you. I am yours. We belong to one another.

These were the words he longed to speak, but he did not want to frighten her with the depth of his feelings.

So he tried to express himself with the brush of his lips against her belly, the gentleness of his hands as he removed her shorts and underthings.

11

SAGE

Sage trembled with anticipation as she looked up at the wood plank ceiling.

Although she knew this was all real, it felt dreamlike.

Maybe because she had dreamed of surrendering to him so many times.

As good as her dreams were, none of them had anything on this.

She gasped as she felt his breath against the tender skin of her inner thigh.

Sage had never liked this kind of thing. Men in general did *not* know what they were doing down there. And this one especially could not possibly know what to do. Riggs's inexperience made the idiot she'd done this with in college seem like an international playboy in comparison.

But she was feverish with honeyed desire. It seemed her whole happiness began and ended with the places he touched her - a hand on her thigh, lips against her skin.

She felt she could come apart at a thought. Or not come apart at all and not care.

She only knew that she needed his touch more than she needed her next breath.

His big hands parted her sex.

"Oh, Sage," he groaned.

She actually felt her body respond at the sound. She was pulsing, opening like a flower seeking the sun.

When he pressed his lips to her opening she cried out helplessly.

He growled and stretched his mouth over her, licking and sucking as if he wanted to consume her.

Sage felt her hips lifting off the table to meet his mouth.

He slid a finger against her, teasing as he lapped at her.

She sank her fingernails into the wooden table.

He groaned against her and pressed his finger inside slowly, so slowly.

Sage whimpered, her thighs shaking.

He eased his finger in and out slowly, massaging her interior in a way that made her eyes roll back.

"Please," she keened, astonished to hear herself beg.

Instantly he strummed her clitoris with his tongue, his fingers playing the rhythm she needed inside.

Sage cried out and then the world seemed to explode behind her eyelids, shooting stars pulsing in time with her pleasure.

Riggs continued to toy with her until the stimulation was too much and she tugged at his hands, urging him up to her.

He crawled up onto the table top with her. His eyes were shining with wonder, though his jaw was taut with need.

Sage reached down to unbutton his jeans.

He pushed her hands away gently.

"Don't you want...?" she hardly had to finish the question. What he wanted was clear by his expression and the outrageously large bulge in his pants.

But he shook his head.

"That was incredible," he murmured. "It was all I need."

"It was not all you need," she protested.

"It is all I need for now," he said calmly, resting on his side beside her.

He placed a hand on her chest, and closed his eyes, as if he were trying to feel her heart beat.

"I have never felt such happiness," he whispered.

She put her hand over his and smiled. She felt happy too. But also loose-limbed and sleepy.

"You're tired, aren't you?" he asked, chuckling.

She nodded.

"Why don't you rest a little?" he asked. "I'll wake you when it's time to finish the sign."

"It does need to dry before we letter it," she said over a tremendous yawn.

He leaned down to kiss her forehead.

The last thing she remembered before falling asleep was the pleasant sensation of his hand stroking her hair.

.

12

RIGGS

L ater that night, Riggs looked across the candlelit dinner table at his beloved mate.

She was smiling and laughing with Tansy and Arden, but he knew that some part of her was sharing the happiness he felt, a happiness that was theirs alone.

He had finished painting the sign while she napped in the mess hall. Then he had woken her and they had walked through the woods back to the truck.

Sage drove back to the farm as Riggs sang love songs to her that made her giggle because they were from 80s movies. But it was good-natured giggling and after all, Riggs *had* had the time of his life. When she joined in the songs he knew things were going to be okay.

More than that, they were going to be wonderful.

They arrived at home to find that the others had cooked dinner. It was not as delicious as Sage's meals, but it was tasty. And Otis had made a peach crumble for dessert.

"So you guys really hung up fifty flyers today?" Tansy asked, sounding impressed.

"Yes," Sage said. "And I have to give Riggs most of the credit. He really knows how to talk to people."

Burton elbowed Riggs.

Riggs smiled and looked down at his plate.

"So what kind of flyers are these?" Arden asked.

"Just a simple thing letting people know where to come and our hours and all," Tansy said. "Same ones Grandma Helen used for years."

"Actually..." Sage began.

"You didn't?" Tansy exclaimed.

Sage shrugged.

"Show me right now," Tansy said.

"What's this?" Arden asked.

"Sage is a natural marketer," Tansy said. "I've been begging her to revamp the farm's image, but she insists she's an accountant."

"I am literally an accountant," Sage protested.

"No more talking, I want to see the flyer," Tansy said. "Please don't tell me you hung *all* of them up."

"There are a few more in the truck," Riggs said, getting up.

Sage gave him a look that told him he wasn't supposed to have shared that news.

"Don't get up," Arden told him. "I'll grab them."

She was halfway to the door before he could protest, so he sat back down.

Sage smiled at him from across the table and his heart ached with joy. She was so beautiful it almost hurt to look at her.

The front door slammed open.

Everyone turned to see Arden standing in the doorway looking shell-shocked.

"Arden," Drago said, leaping to his feet.

"I think you need to come outside," Arden said. Her voice was tight.

Everyone got up. Riggs waited for Sage at the door. His protective instincts were kicking into overdrive. He didn't like the idea of her going out to see whatever had made Arden's face go pale.

But the look of determination on his mate's face told him he need not waste his efforts trying to keep her away.

They followed Arden and Drago across the front porch and down to the gravel driveway, with Tansy and Burton bringing up the rear.

"Look," Arden said.

She was pointing at the tractor, which was parked close to the truck.

Something was wrong with its tires. They appeared to have melted into the ground.

"The tires are melted," Drago breathed, echoing Riggs's thought.

"No," Arden said. "They're flat. Or I should say, they're slashed."

"No," Tansy breathed.

Riggs noticed something in the mud beside the drive. He bent to take a closer look.

It was footprints, but something about them was off. There was an indentation between the big toe and the rest of the toes on each print. Riggs knew he'd seen something like this before, but he couldn't put his finger on it.

"Ninjas," his brother Drago shouted, making the connection before Riggs could.

Of course. How could he have missed it? Everyone knew that ninjas wore special boots that left this type of mark.

"What?" Sage asked, moving to join him.

"Oh, yeah, those are definitive," Burton agreed.

"This is very bad," Drago said. "We must get our mates to safety and then prepare for battle."

"What are you talking about?" Arden demanded.

"This farm is under attack by ninja warriors," Drago announced.

Riggs's heart was beating a mile a minute. He wrapped a protective arm around Sage and scanned their surroundings.

But the setting sun cast shadows everywhere, it was nearly impossible to tell the difference between a man and a shrub in this light.

Besides, everyone knew ninjas were masters of deception. There could be ten of them here now, hiding themselves in the trees and grass, ready to spring forth into action at any moment.

"What could you have done to get yourselves on the wrong side of ninjas?" Burton worried out loud.

"Okay, enough already," Tansy said. "I think I understand what's going on."

"You do?" Sage asked.

"There are tons of ninjas in the movies, especially in '80s movies," Tansy said patiently. "But ninjas are not really a problem anymore, not for hundreds of years. I mean, they never really were. At least not in rural Pennsylvania."

"Then how do you explain the prints, Tansy?" Drago asked, not looking even a little bit convinced.

"The person who left those prints knows about ninjas the same way you do, from the movies," Tansy said. "It's just some idiot in a karate suit."

"We know what we must do then," Riggs said, determined to make things right.

"What?" Sage asked, looking mystified.

"We'll find his dojo," Riggs said.

"And we'll challenge him!" Drago finished.

"Oh, no, that's not how it's done," Tansy said, suppressing most of a smile.

"We know how this is done," Burton said.

"Look, whoever it is, they are just trying to scare us," Tansy said.

"Trying to *sabotage* us," Sage suggested.

"The same person who vandalized the sign?" Riggs wondered out loud.

"What do you mean vandalized the sign?" Tansy asked.

"Oh, no," Riggs said, realizing that he had just given away his secret with Sage. "I'm so sorry, Tansy. I didn't want to upset you. But someone vandalized the peach picking sign.

He looked to his mate and she shrugged.

He was grateful that she wasn't mad.

But Tansy was weeping.

"Do not worry, Tansy," Riggs said, feeling terrible. "Sage and I have fixed the sign."

But Tansy didn't even look up.

"Tansy, are you okay?" Burton asked.

"I noticed something too," she said, her words muffled by her hands, which still covered her face.

They all waited.

Tansy wiped her cheeks and looked up at the little group.

"This morning when I got up I found a dead rabbit on the steps," she said. "Cleo leaves me a mouse or a mole sometimes, but this seemed too big to be one of her presents. And its throat was slashed, probably by something more powerful than her claws. I didn't want to upset anyone..."

She put her hands to her face again and Burton wrapped his arms around her.

Sage met Riggs's eye from across the circle of friends.

She wore a mask of fierce determination that sent a shiver down his spine.

Riggs glanced around again. If the ninja was watching and saw that look, he was probably shaking in his funny little boots.

13

CLEM

Clement Peterson came in the front door whistling and threw his hat on the kitchen table along with the six-pack of beer he'd bought on the way home.

Today was a special day, so he'd splurged on the good stuff from the fancy organic grocer in town.

He opened the fridge to see if there was anything good in there.

There wasn't.

"You get beer?" Gretchen yelled from the living room.

He could hear *Nailed It* playing in the background. All of his sister's favorite shows were ones where there was a chance for people to get humiliated.

"Yeah," he called back to her.

Normally he tried to get home before Gretchen. He liked having control of the remote and the good spot on the couch.

But tonight he was glad she was there. He had been dying to tell her everything he'd done.

He snatched the six-pack off the table and headed out to join her.

"Ha, I can't believe you got that girlie stuff again," Gretchen said, eying the beer as he placed it on the coffee table.

"It's not girlie," he told her. "It's called Framboise, and it's from Belgium."

"I rest my case," she said. "Besides, anything that comes from that frou-frou store in town is all organic, free-range bullshit."

He scowled at her.

"It has raspberries on the label," she added, her contempt not preventing her from grabbing the first bottle out of the pack and popping the top against the edge of the coffee table to open it.

"Men eat raspberries," Clem said, opening his own can. "Besides, this is kind of a celebration."

"Oh yeah?" Gretchen took her eyes off the beer and straightened up, paying attention to him for once.

"What did you do?" Her mischievous eyes flashed with glee.

He took a big swallow, building her anticipation a little.

"Well, first thing this morning I shot a rabbit, slit its throat, and left it on their doorstep," he said, grinning at the thought of one of those girls waking up to find it there.

"Gross," Gretchen said. "Okay."

"And I painted on their pick-your-own-peaches sign," he said.

"What do you mean you painted on it?" she asked.

"I turned 'Martin's Bounty' into 'Martian's Booty'," he said, snickering.

"Okay, I get it," Gretchen said. "I guess."

"And I went over around dinner time and slashed the tires of their tractor," he added, waiting for her reaction.

She nodded, but way less enthusiastically than he'd expected.

Maybe she would have been more impressed if she had seen how cool he'd looked decked out in all the ninja gear he'd accumulated over the years. Gretchen had always told him it was a waste of money, but she no idea how quiet he'd been in his tabi boots, or how easily he'd punctured the tractor tires with his tanto dagger.

No appreciation for the finer things in life – that was her problem.

"And then I cut the brake line on it," he said.

That had been his finishing touch. Cutting the brakes on someone's actual car might have been going too far. But all that was going to happen with the tractor was that one of them was going to end up driving it into a ditch, or right into the cornfield. That would be epic.

"That's a little better," Gretchen said, raising one eyebrow. "What else?"

"What do you mean *what else?*" he spluttered. "I barely had time to *do* anything else between that and work."

"What the hell, Clem?" Gretchen hollered, slapping him with a throw pillow. "This isn't some senior prank. This is serious. There's a lot of money at stake."

Typical Gretchen.

"I'm in charge now," he stormed, totally losing his cool. "You fucked up with the bees and dad put *me* in charge."

"You may be in charge, but you need to step it up or we won't get rid of them in time," Gretchen spat. "That guy wants to start construction before winter."

The phone rang, interrupting their argument.

Gretchen looked at Clem like she was the Queen of

Sheba and picking up the landline was beneath her. Whatever.

Clem got up and grabbed the receiver off the cradle.

"Petersons'," he said into it.

"It's Dolly," the woman on the other end said. "Put your daddy on."

It was funny, all his life Dolly Strickland had seemed like Mrs. Santa Claus to Clem. He never suspected she had a heart of ice.

"He's at Rotary," Clem replied. "But, uh, I can report if you want."

There was a momentary silence.

"Put her on speaker," Gretchen yelled.

"Yes, dear, put me on speaker so I can hear what your sister has to say," Dolly agreed, sounding relieved that there was another Peterson around for her to talk with.

Clem might not be a big talker, but that didn't mean he couldn't get down to business.

He put her on speaker anyway, then placed the receiver on the coffee table and sat next to his sister on the sofa.

"Roman Panchenko called me today about his space casino," Dolly said, sounding a little shaken. "Do I have news for him?"

Clem swallowed, suddenly getting his sister's point about his plans being small time.

"I started with some vandalism, intimidation, a bit of property destruction," Clem said. "I didn't get caught either."

"Did they even notice it?" Dolly asked. "I didn't see any police activity over there today."

Damn. He hadn't thought of that.

"Listen," Dolly said. "I told Roman Panchenko personally that your family would help make the land available for his alien-themed casino."

Clem swallowed. Rumor had it that the Panchenko guy was linked to the mob out in Glacier City. He was no one to be messed with.

"I don't like to think about what could happen if you fail to follow through," Dolly said, echoing his own fears. "Do you?"

Clem wasn't sure how to respond.

"Of course not," Gretchen said, breaking Clem's silence. "We're gonna think bigger."

"The key with them is money," Dolly said. "We want to make sure no one goes near those peaches of theirs. Then they won't be able to afford to hold onto the place and they'll have to sell."

"How do we do that?" Clem asked, mystified.

"What does everyone in this town hate?" Dolly asked. "Figure that out, and find a way to link it to their peaches and you've got it all lined up."

"What does everyone hate?" Clem echoed.

"I dunno," Gretchen said. "This place is getting so fruity lately. Gluten? Tree nuts? Any crap they don't sell at that fancy grocery store."

"That's ridiculous," Clem said.

"No," Dolly said. "No, I think you're on to something here. Gluten-free, free range, non-GMO..."

"What the hell is a GMO?" Clem asked.

"It's perfect," Dolly said reverently. "GMOs are genetically modified organisms. If we spread that rumor, it will check out. Those peaches over on Martin's Bounty bloom way earlier than anywhere else around here."

"But their peaches have always ripened early," Clem

said. "It's one of the reasons they've always been such big seller."

"And this year, it will be the reason they fail. Remember, it doesn't have to be true," Dolly said slowly, as if he were stupid. "It just has to be enough to scare people away."

"Holy shit," Gretchen breathed. "Clem, when we sabotaged the water there were no blooms on those trees. And now there are ripe peaches?"

Clem thought about it. She was right. That did seem too fast. He stared at her, his mind buzzing a mile a minute to work it out.

"How did they do that?" he asked.

"Doesn't matter," Dolly said.

"It just has to scare people away," Gretchen said, her eyes lighting up with pleasure.

Clem was starting to think he wasn't going to get a chance to use his grapping hook after all.

14

RIGGS

R iggs paced the floor of the barn after dinner.
He could feel Drago and Burton's eyes on him, their concern palpable.

He wanted to obey Sage's wishes and handle things in the way she thought was right.

But he knew what had to be done.

"That's it," he said, stopping suddenly. "I'm going."

"Where?" Drago asked.

"I saw a sign for the town karate studio when I was in the village today," Riggs said. "There's a class going on right now at the community center. I'm going to find the person who did this. And I'm going to challenge him."

"This is what I hoped you would say," Drago exclaimed, clapping him on the back. "I will join you, brother."

"So will I," Burton added.

Riggs was relieved at the thought of having his brothers along, but didn't want to get them in hot water with their mates.

"The women will not be pleased," Riggs warned. "Maybe it's best if I go alone."

"No," Drago said, his blue eyes flashing.

"And miss the ninjas?" Burton asked. "No way. We're coming too."

"Let's leave a note for them," Riggs suggested. "We won't be back to make s'mores tonight. And we don't want them to worry."

Drago nodded and sat at the makeshift desk in the corner. He grabbed paper and pen and began to laboriously write a note.

"Do we need weapons, brother?" Burton asked. His dark eyes were so solemn.

"I do not think so," Riggs said. "Karate is a sport of honor. I will fight bare-handed."

"We will stand beside you, brother," Burton said worriedly.

"Okay," Drago announced, folding the paper and placing it in his pocket. "I'll slip this under the door on our way out."

"How will we get there?" Burton asked. "There are only two horses."

"We'll take the truck," Riggs laughed.

"You can drive it?" Burton sounded amazed.

"I flew our spacecraft, Burton, and I rode around in the car with Sage all day today," Riggs reminded him patiently. "It's a fairly simple contraption. The combustion engine is woefully inefficient and terribly noisy, but relatively safe."

"What about the keys?" Drago asked.

"The keys are under the floor mat," Riggs said.

"These women are too trusting," Drago muttered.

"They have us now, they don't have to worry about protecting themselves," Burton said proudly.

"Still, they should secure their vehicle," Drago said. "Especially with ninjas afoot."

He snuck off to the front porch and slipped his note in the door slot, then jogged to meet them by the truck.

The three of them barely fit on the bench seat.

Riggs started up the truck and they headed down the gravel driveway, the machine proving as easy to operate as he had hoped.

"Where is the community center?" Burton asked.

"It's in town, just a few minutes away," Riggs replied.

He knew why Burton was asking. His own bond to Sage was not yet secured and yet he felt the growing physical distance between them stretching him tight already. He could only imagine how his brothers must feel, leaving their bonded mates behind.

The road curved past trees and homes and eventually carried them into town. Riggs found the community center and parked outside. It was a large brick building. The windows glowed with warm light.

The three brothers slid out of the cab of the truck and headed for the door.

Riggs took a deep breath and pushed it open.

He expected to be entering a lobby. Instead he walked into the middle of a karate class.

An enormous open arena was lined with brightly colored mats. Two evenly spaced rows of people wearing white uniforms stared at him.

"Welcome," a friendly voice said.

A small man with brown skin and a uniform with billowing black pants approached him, smiling.

"I'm Sensei Rick," he said, extending his hand.

Riggs took it instinctively and shook.

"So you're interested in studying aikido?" Sensei Rick asked.

"I'm here because someone has been vandalizing our...

friends' farm," Riggs said. "And we have reason to believe it was someone from this school."

He looked around the room, treating its occupants to a withering glare.

The students on the mats stared back at him, thunderstruck. They looked surprisingly nonthreatening.

Sensei Rick placed a hand on his shoulder.

"I'm sorry to hear about the farm," he said kindly. "I know Helen Martin just passed. It's good to know the Martin girls have friends looking out for them. But I don't think any of my students would have vandalized their farm."

"You are dangerous ninjas," Drago said, stepping forward. "Who else would have done it?"

"No, son, this is an aikido class," Sensei Rick said. "Aikido is the way of the harmonious spirit."

"The way of the harmonious spirit?" Drago echoed.

Sensei Rick pointed at the wall.

A framed poster said:

"LOYALTY AND DEVOTION *lead to bravery.*
        Bravery leads to the spirit of self-sacrifice.
        Self-sacrifice creates trust in the power of love."
        - Morihei Ueshiba (founder of aikido)

SOMETHING about the words made Riggs think instantly of Aerie, and he felt a warmth in his chest.

"How can you beat people up with that?" Drago asked.

"We do not beat people up at all," Sensei Rick laughed. "But if an assailant should attack us, we restore them to harmony."

Riggs blinked at him.

"How exactly would you do that?" Burton asked doubtfully.

"Would you like a demonstration?" Sensei Rick asked.

"Yes," Riggs said.

"What's your name, son?" Sensei Rick asked him.

"It's Riggs," he said.

"Students," Sensei Rick said. "This is Riggs. He and his friends are interested in knowing more about aikido. Have a seat and we're going to do a little demonstration."

A murmur of shy hellos chorused up to Riggs as the students seated themselves on the mats.

The friendly atmosphere got the better of him, and he gave a little wave.

"Alright, Riggs, let's say I'm walking down the street, minding my own business," Sensei Rick began. "You come up to me and begin a confrontation. For example, you could ask me if I vandalized your friend's farm."

Riggs pulled himself up straight and marched over to Sensei Rick who was walking along the center of the mats, whistling.

"Did you vandalize my friend's farm?" Riggs asked.

"Now, right here I have a choice to make," Sensei Rick said, turning to his students. "I can choose to escalate the situation or I can choose the way of peace."

"I want no trouble," he said, turning back to Riggs with his hands up. "Can we talk about this?"

Riggs stared at him, wondering what he was supposed to do next.

"Now, let's say he backs down and agrees to talk with me," Sensei Rick said to the class. "We can talk as we just did and make a connection. We have harmony."

There were nods and murmurs of assent.

"But," Sensei Rick said, "what if he doesn't want to talk?"

Sensei Rick's eyebrows went up so high they nearly reached his hairline.

"Okay, son, grab my wrist and try and pull me in for a fight," he said to Riggs.

Riggs looked at Sensei Rick.

He was a small man, practically child-sized compared to Riggs's enormous form. And he was older than Riggs, much older.

It did not feel right to grab him.

"Really, son, it's okay, just grab my wrist and pull," Sensei Rick encouraged him.

Riggs grabbed Sensei Rick's wrist and gave a tug.

Instantly, Riggs found himself flying through the air.

He landed on the mats with a mighty thump.

The students applauded politely as he got to his feet, still breathless with surprise. He did not seem to be hurt at all.

"And now he is restored to harmony," Sensei Rick said in a pleased way. "Great job, Riggs."

"I want to try," Drago said immediately.

"Of course, you can all give it a try," Sensei Rick said. "I just need you to sign some waivers for me. Evelyn, lead the warm-up while I get these guys set up for their free class."

Sensei Rick placed a hand on Riggs's arm and led him toward a desk in the corner of the room. The other men trailed behind.

"I hope you'll enjoy the lesson tonight," he told Riggs. "And if there is anything I can do as far as the situation on Helen's farm, I'll be glad to help. We can talk about it after class."

Riggs was sure he would not find their vandal among these people, but he was beginning to think maybe their visit would not be a total loss.

15

SAGE

S age stepped into the living room with a bowl of marshmallows and noticed a piece of paper on the floor near the front door.

She placed the bowl on the table and bent to retrieve the note. It was folded and had *Arden* scrawled on it.

"Arden," she called.

Her friend came out of the kitchen at just that moment, carrying a plate of chocolate.

"What is it?" Arden asked.

Sage handed her the paper as Tansy came in with a box of graham crackers.

Arden unfolded it and began to read as Sage watched.

"Holy crap," she murmured.

"What is it?" Sage asked.

Arden handed it to her instead of answering.

DEAR ARDEN,

We are very sorry to miss evening s'mores with you and Tansy and Sage.

My brothers and I are going to the karate dojo to challenge the enemy who dishonored the farm. We know you don't agree, but the films we studied explain that this is a "guy" thing that women must object to. And they showed us that standing up to bullies is the only way to gain their respect.

Do not fear, my beautiful mate. By the time you read this everything will be taken care of. We were created to be strong and fierce.

Love,

Drago

"A GUY THING?" Sage huffed. "That women *must* object to?"

"Keep in mind that they learned everything they know from '80s movies," Arden said carefully.

"I'll give it to them - it is a classic plot," Tansy said. "But they're barking up the wrong tree if they're going to Rick Johnson for answers. He's literally the nicest man in this town."

"At least he won't hurt them," Arden said. "And you have to admit, it's pretty brave of them if they think they're really going after ninjas or Cobra Kai or something."

"How can you two react like this?" Sage demanded, throwing the note on the table. "What they've done is nothing more than stupid machismo."

"Come on, Sage," Tansy said. "You don't really think that, do you? I'm not convinced they even know what machismo is."

"I don't care if they know what it is or not. This is too much," Sage stormed. "Everything about them is just too much."

"Not too much for us, Sage," Tansy said quietly.

Sage looked up at her sister and Arden. They observed her solemnly, sadly.

"Well, it might be too much for me," she told them gently.

"Just give him a chance," Tansy pleaded.

"I got the school tax bill today," Sage replied. "It's higher than last year, way higher. I called to see if it was a mistake. They said they're building a new middle school. It will have state-of-the-art computer and science labs."

"That's fantastic," Arden said, then clapped her hand over her mouth as if remembering the first part of what Sage had said.

"It is fantastic," Sage agreed. "But we were already scraping to figure out how to cover the taxes at the level they were last year. And how to pay the insurance, and all the supplies we'll need for the fall season."

Tansy lowered her face to her hands.

It hurt Sage's heart every time her sister had to face reality about the farm finances. It didn't seem to matter how many times they had the conversation, Tansy's reaction was always as emotional as the first time.

"We have so many problems from every side," Sage said gently. "And the vandalism was bad, but if we have fugitive aliens running off to beat someone up every time something goes wrong... Well, that makes our money situation seem easy to deal with."

"Should we go after them?" Arden asked.

"In what?" Sage asked. "The tractor with the slashed tires?"

"They *drove*?" Arden asked, running to the window.

"Well, I hope they did," Sage said. "The truck is gone."

"I'm getting the sangria," Tansy said through a clenched jaw.

"I'd rather have tea," Sage said. "I want to have my wits about me when these bozos get back."

16

RIGGS

R iggs burst in the front door of the farmhouse, his brothers piling in behind him.

"It was amazing," he said to Sage, who was seated on a large cushion on the floor.

"You're back," she said flatly.

"Did you find out anything about the vandal?" Tansy asked.

"No, but Tansy, you have to try aikido," Burton exclaimed. "Come over here and grab my wrist."

"No, no," Drago said. "We have to tell them about peace and harmony first."

"You were at a karate class, not a UN Summit," Tansy said.

"The art of peace is the principle of nonresistance," Burton replied.

"The true meaning of 'samurai' is one who serves and adheres to the power of love," Drago added.

"Just grab my wrist, so I can restore you to harmony," Riggs said to Sage. "Please?"

Sage slammed her mug down on the table, not seeming

to notice that tea sloshed over the sides, and leapt to
her feet.

It occurred to Riggs that in his excitement, he may have
failed to properly predict Sage's reaction.

"Look," she growled. "We have problems, real problems.
And you three take off without even talking to us about it.
Then you come waltzing back, spouting platitudes, asking
us to grab your wrists without a care in the world. You don't
worry about the fact that you just drove a car without a
license. Or that you just appeared, all three of you together,
in very public place, where you might have been recognized
for what you are. You put everyone in this room at risk of jail
for harboring a fugitive, or worse."

Riggs felt her words as if she had punched him in
the chest.

The worst of it was that she was right. He'd been so
eager to save the day, he hadn't thought about the possible
consequences of his actions.

"I-I'm sorry, Sage, I—" he began.

"Good," she said. "I'm glad you're sorry. I'm sorry too. I'm
sorry that I was stupid enough to believe that a man who
has only been emulating a human for a couple of months
would have the common sense the good lord promised a
house plant."

The room was deadly silent.

"I'm going to bed," Sage said.

She stalked down the hallway toward her room.

Riggs lowered himself to the sofa and rested his head in
his hands.

"Riggs," Tansy said. "She doesn't mean it. She's just
stressed out."

"No," he said, straightening up. "She's one hundred
percent right. I don't know what I was thinking."

"I know what you were thinking," Arden said gently. "You were thinking that you love her and you want to protect her."

Riggs nodded, afraid to try to speak.

"She knows that," Tansy said, patting his back.

"I'm not so sure," Riggs said.

"Give her time," Tansy said. "Let her cool off, things will look better in the morning."

He nodded, not wanting to contradict Tansy, whom he liked very much.

"I think I'll just go for a walk before bed," he said. "You should all enjoy your dessert. I'll see you in the morning."

"I'll come with you, brother," Burton offered brightly.

"No, thank you," Riggs said. "I think I just need to spend some time alone."

Burton nodded but he looked taken aback.

Riggs understood why his brother was surprised. Ever since they had begun the arduous project of moving into human forms back on Aerie the brothers had been inseparable.

He realized, ruefully, that perhaps this sudden longing for private introspection was a sign that he was becoming more human after all.

"Have a good walk." Drago clapped Riggs on the shoulder as he headed out the door. "And come back for us if you change your mind."

"Thank you, brother," Riggs said.

But he was already gazing out into the starry sky over the berry fields.

The stars were so far away on this planet. Perhaps this was what made him feel so small tonight.

17

SAGE

Sage slipped into her room, pushing down the feeling of dread in her gut that told her she had been too harsh.

Usually when she spoke her mind she felt better afterward. It was the feeling of a sunny morning after a storm.

This time, she felt bone tired and sad.

She curled up in her bed without even getting undressed, staring at the darkened window as she listened to the hushed voices of the others in the living room.

She imagined the tightness she felt in her chest would have her up all night.

But she sank quickly into a deep and dreamless sleep.

The next morning she woke early, feeling disoriented.

For one blessed instant she thought only of the day ahead and how much she could accomplish since she was up at such an ungodly hour.

Then she realized she was still dressed, and the whole night before came crashing into her consciousness.

Get up and go about your business, she told herself sternly.

It would do her no good to worry about the boys' adventure in town. Or the awful things she had said when they returned.

She showered and dressed quickly, then made her way to the kitchen.

Otis, blessedly, had not yet arrived, and she had the room to herself.

She threw on Grandma Helen's favorite apron and set about preparing a big country breakfast.

She wasn't apologizing with it exactly. She had meant every word she said last night. And she certainly was relieved that the men had disabused her of the notion that they could operate properly in the regular Earth world before she ended up mated to Riggs and it was too late.

Her regret centered on her wish that she had been gentler, or reprimanded Riggs privately. Because even if he was an ignorant alien man-child, he was a *nice* ignorant alien man-child.

An image of him leaning down to kiss her invaded her mind and she had to bite her lip hard to stop the surge of need that nearly carried her off.

Just cook.

Preparing a big meal was something constructive to do with her hands and mind. Sage had always used cooking to cope. She and Otis had that in common, as much as she hated to admit it.

She had just gotten into the swing of it with biscuit dough rising and a jar of apple preserves brought up from the cellar when the doorbell rang.

Stunned, Sage checked the clock over the kitchen sink.

It wasn't even six yet.

She wondered if it might be Otis. She didn't think he rang the bell each morning - surely that would wake everyone.

She wiped her hands on the apron and went to the door.

She was stunned to see a newscaster and crew on the other side.

"Hi there, I'm Arlene Wiggins from Channel Eight News," the reporter said. "Are you Sage or Tansy Martin?"

"I'm Sage," Sage said. "What- what's going on?"

But Arlene turned to the cameraman.

"This is Arlene Wiggins from Channel Eight News, here with Sage Martin of Martin's Bounty," she said brightly, then turned to Sage. "Ms. Martin, Channel Eight News received a call on our tip line alerting us to non-disclosed use of GMOs in your peach trees. What do you say to this accusation?"

"GMOs?" Sage echoed, confused.

"Genetically modified organisms," Arlene said slowly. "As you already know, being a farmer."

For a golden instant Sage allowed herself to celebrate the fact that the reporter wasn't here because someone had spotted three hot aliens without a license in a borrowed vehicle returning to the farm last night. Then she came to her senses and shot back at Arlene.

"I'm confused as to why you would even broach this topic in relation to my grandparents' farm," Sage retorted. "If you did your homework, you would know those trees are cuttings of the original peaches planted by my grandfather decades ago. These peaches have been growing on this land since before you knew how to spell GMO."

Tansy wandered into the room looking sleepy and then stunned when she noticed who was outside.

"According to my research, peach trees only produce for twelve years," Arlene said. But her voice was less certain.

"These are non-GMO peaches, Arlene," Sage said. "Go and Google 'cuttings'."

"So you won't have any objection to Channel Eight News independently verifying that?" Arlene shot back.

"Of course not," Sage said. "We have nothing to hide."

"You heard it here first," Arlene said to the camera. "We're heading up to the Martin's Bounty peach orchard to obtain a sample and we'll make sure to keep you up with the test results, every step of the way. For Channel Eight News, I'm Arlene Wiggins."

The cameraman unshouldered his rig and gave her a thumbs-up.

"Thanks, hon', that's great TV," Arlene said to Sage, suddenly sounding friendly now that the cameras were off. "We'll ring the bell again when we have test results. Keep the apron - that's a nice touch, but eighty-six the ponytail. Viewers want women to look feminine."

"Get out," Sage said, clenching her jaw to keep herself from saying more.

"But I can take my sample, right?" Arlene asked.

Sage nodded.

Wiggins and her crew headed toward the peaches.

Tansy put a hand on Sage's shoulder. They watched as Arlene snagged a peach from one of the trees and held it up to Sage, as if in toast. One of the crew handed her a ziplock bag and she tucked it in the bag in her purse.

The crew trailed her down the hillside and into the news van that was parked on the gravel drive.

The whole thing was surreal.

They were still standing there when Arden sprinted toward the house, Drago and Riggs in her wake.

"What was that about?" Arden asked, panting, her eyes wide.

"Oh, nothing about the men," Sage said. "Some idiot

called their tip line and said our peaches were genetically modified."

"What did you tell them?" Arden asked.

"I told them the peaches were not genetically modified," Sage said slowly, wondering what she was missing.

"Why did they take one?" Drago asked.

"Oh, they wanted to test it," Sage said with a shrug. "They won't find anything. Can you believe the nerve of them? Coming here with cameras rolling and literally nothing but a bad tip?"

"Sage, Tansy, I think you should sit down," Arden said.

Sage felt a wash of ice water through her veins, though she had no idea what Arden could possibly say that would make things worse.

She sat and Tansy sat beside her.

"You know how the trees weren't blooming?" Arden asked.

"Yes, and you realized there was poison in their water supply," Sage said.

"Did you notice how quickly the trees bounced back?" Arden asked.

Sage blinked.

"Yes," Tansy said quietly.

"Would you have expected them to bloom so quickly?" Arden asked.

Sage turned to Tansy.

Tansy bit her lip and shook her head. "The fruit always comes early and ripens quickly, though this year it happened exceptionally quickly. But I've definitely never seen the trees blossom suddenly like that. I thought it might have something to do with the water."

"Oh god, you think she'll find traces of the chemical in the peaches?" Sage asked.

"No," Arden said. "Thankfully that's not an issue, or we wouldn't be selling the peaches at all. There's something else... special about these peaches."

Riggs began to pace in front of the window, she'd never seen him so anxious about anything.

Arden looked to Drago, who nodded solemnly. Burton placed a hand on Tansy's shoulder.

"Something you don't know yet about these men is that they each have a little something extra," Arden said. "A gift - maybe a remnant of their old life on Aerie."

"What do you mean *a gift*?" Sage asked.

"Drago's gift has to do with plants," Arden said. "He can commune with plant life."

"You mean he has a green thumb?" Sage asked.

"I'll show you," Drago offered. "It will be easier than trying to explain."

He moved to the window and took down a small pot with an African violet in it. It was a tiny thing, a few fuzzy leaves, fuller on the side that faced the exterior than on the other. It had been in the window ever since Sage could remember.

Drago knelt in front of Sage, holding the little plant out between them.

He closed his eyes.

At first nothing happened. A slight breeze in the room moved the curtains.

Then the plant transformed before Sage's eyes.

The leaves unfurled, a deep, lush green. Buds appeared and burst into bloom, a glorious purple against the background of fuzzy green leaves.

Drago opened his eyes and smiled down at the little plant.

"Y-you made it grow," Sage stammered.

"No," he said, shaking his head. "I asked it to grow."

Sage looked to Arden in question.

Arden nodded.

"This is why the peaches bloomed," Tansy said to Drago, nodding her head slowly, a look of dawning admiration on her face. "You did this."

"We did it," he said, glancing over at Arden.

"How exactly does it work?" Tansy asked. "Scientifically, I mean."

"We don't know," Arden said. "This is why I don't like that they're testing the fruit."

"But you didn't put anything into it," Tansy said.

"True," Arden agreed. "But communicating with a plant at this level, supporting it, pushing it to bloom, surely there could be chemical changes at some level. Maybe even something that would raise a red flag on the tests they are about to do."

Sage leapt up from the sofa.

Her sudden movement sent Drago sprawling backward, and he nearly dropped the violet.

"Tansy," she said, turning to her sister.

But Tansy's expression was one of wonder and excitement.

Sage was reeling. Yet her sister sat there, calmly taking it all in without a single question.

"Tansy, this isn't normal," she heard herself say, her voice higher pitched than usual.

Tansy nodded up at her. Concern drew down the corners of her lips, but it was clear as day to Sage that she was more worried about *her* than about the madness she had just witnessed.

Then it hit Sage. Tansy was mated to Burton. She was

already in too deep. If these things that looked like men could make plants obey them...

"What have we gotten ourselves into?" Sage moaned.

Her stomach clenched and she pushed past Arden and ran out the front door.

18

RIGGS

R iggs bolted out the front door and ran after Sage, his heart pounding with dread.

He caught up to her under the sycamore that overlooked the berry fields.

"Sage," he called to her.

"No," she said, walking faster. "I can't."

"Wait, please," he said. "Can we just talk for a minute?"

She spun around, fixing him with her dark eyes.

"There's no point, Riggs," she said. "What's done is done."

"Whatever that test result shows, we can still sell the peaches," Riggs said, reaching for a solution. "Maybe we sell them to scientists instead of tourists if there's something unusual about them."

"It's not just the peaches, Riggs, and you know it," she countered.

"You mean our relationship," he said sadly. "Dr. Bhimani warned us not to demonstrate our gifts until after we had a mate bond. She said it would make us seem more alien to humans."

"She's right, it does make you seem more alien," Sage said. "It never occurred to any of you that it would only be fair to share that with us before we were mated to you *forever*?"

"I, uh, never thought about that," Riggs admitted.

"Do you all have gifts?" Sage asked. "Burton and... you?"

He nodded.

He was ready to tell her about his gift, to tell her anything she wanted to know. He would gladly rip open his chest and show her his aching heart if she wanted to see it.

But she merely nodded, lips buttoned tightly.

"I care about you, Sage," he said. "Please don't push me out of your life."

"I'm true to my word. We won't kick you off the farm," she said.

"That's not what I meant," he told her gently.

"I won't be involved with you on a personal level," she said. "And as far as the farm, we're going to have to sell soon anyway, with or without the stupid peaches."

"You won't have to sell the farm," Riggs told her. "I'll work harder. We all will."

"I've done the math, Riggs," she said simply. "Even if we had our best year ever, the tourists would have to pay twice what the fruit is worth for us to catch up enough to be ready for next year. And we'd be lucky to get half the traffic the farm usually gets. The only thing anyone in this town wants to visit is aliens."

He nodded. Sage was an accountant. If she said the farm wouldn't work, then it wouldn't. He did not envy her having to break this news to Tansy.

"I really just want a few minutes alone to get some fresh air," Sage said softly.

"I'll be right inside if you need me," Riggs said.

She nodded but he heard her thoughts as clearly as if she had said them out loud.

I won't.

19

CLEM

C lement Peterson stood in a cramped hallway in the Channel Eight news building in Stargazer.

The newsroom always looked so fancy on the air. He'd never really pictured threadbare carpets, fluorescent lights and people running around with styrofoam coffee cups backstage.

"You the one waiting for Arlene?" a guy with a clipboard and an anxious look asked him.

Clem nodded.

"Follow me," the guy said.

Clem followed him about ten feet down the hallway and then the guy knocked on a door.

"Come in," Arlene sang out. Her rural Pennsylvania twang made her sound like one of Clem's aunts. He didn't know why he'd assumed the way she talked on the news was how she really talked.

"Hey, uh, I'm the guy who sent in the tip about the peaches at Martin's Bounty," he said.

"Oh shit, yeah, come on in," Arlene said.

The door opened and he almost took a step back.

Arlene's face was covered in some white substance. Her hair was twisted in foam curlers. She looked kind of like Medusa in the comic books Clem read when he was a kid.

He entered the small room. There were two stools in front of a make-up mirror and a rack of women's suits in every color of the rainbow.

"Sit if you want," Arlene said. "But this won't take long."

Clem sat on the stool next to hers. It was on wheels. It took enormous effort on his part not to spin it around.

"Did you test the peaches?" he asked.

"We did," she said. "They're super high in vitamin C, like off the charts. But otherwise they're completely normal. Your tip was useless."

"But that's impossible," he said.

"What makes you think they're genetically modified trees?" Arlene asked, making a strange face in the mirror as she used a sponge to rub the white stuff into her skin.

"I was there two weeks ago and there were no blooms on the trees," Clem said. "And now there are ripe peaches."

Arlene sat up straight and lowered her sponge.

"Now *that's* something," she said. "Can anyone corroborate that?"

"Uh, my sister," he said.

"Not family," Arlene said, shaking her head.

Clem thought of Otis, but there was no way the guy would inform on the Martins. He was practically their butler these days.

"Wait," Clem said.

Arlene raised an eyebrow.

"The cops can," he said. "They got called in when the Martins's bees went missing."

"You think they'd have pictures?" Arlene asked, her eyes sparkling.

"They might," Clem said hopefully.

"We'll check it out." Arlene nodded enthusiastically, her curlers bobbing along with her.

Clem headed out, hoping for the first time in his life that the Stargazer cops had actually done their jobs.

20

SAGE

S age spent the rest of the day avoiding Riggs.

When the men were in the field with the horses, she picked berries. When they moved to the pond for lunch, she went up to the peach orchard and organized the bushel baskets and fruit pickers. When they arrived at the orchard to lay extra gravel on the paths, she headed to the kitchen to prepare dinner.

Sage had wanted to make chicken stew and Otis was pulling for apple pie. They compromised on a menu of chicken pot pie and cold apple cider. Otis was pulling the pies out of the oven when the men came back from swimming in the pond.

Sage was just washing up at the sink. She tried hard and failed not to stare as the three dripping and gorgeous aliens walked past the window in front of her.

Riggs was resplendent, shirtless and unselfconscious. The afternoon sun set the drops of water running down his muscled chest flashing like diamonds. His dark hair hung low over his blue eyes.

When he glanced up at the window, she dropped the

glass measuring cup she was holding into the sink with a clatter.

"Shoot," she exclaimed.

"You okay?" Otis asked.

"I'm fine," she said too fast.

He eyed her suspiciously.

"What?" she asked lightly, turning back to the sink.

"Oh, I don't know," he said politely. "You're just kind of quieter than usual today."

What he meant was that she wasn't carping after him constantly about which utensil to use or how he stirred the broth.

"I'm just tired," she said.

"Okay, I hope you feel... more rested soon," he said. His voice was a bit deeper than usual. He was actually concerned.

She turned and gave him a genuine smile.

For all that he had conspired against her family, he really did feel bad about what he had done.

She allowed herself five seconds to wish she had the good sense to fall in love with someone as refreshingly normal and reassuringly goofy as Otis Rogers. He was a real help in the kitchen.

Unfortunately she didn't want to think about spending time with him in any other room.

The image of wet, half-naked Riggs flashed in her memory and she bit her lip and forced herself to remember what he really was. He might be attractive, but he was an alien. And his judgment was terrible.

The pretty ones are never the sharpest, she heard Howard Gillespie from the print shop say again.

Maybe Howard was right after all.

Arden poked her head into the kitchen.

"Hey Sage," Arden said. "I was going to turn on the news if that's okay?"

"Sure," Sage said. Channel Eight's evening news had started a few minutes ago.

She didn't really want to see herself on camera, but it was important to know what was going out to the public.

She arrived in the living room and joined Arden on the sofa as Arlene Wiggins's face filled the television screen. She was already talking about Martin's Bounty. They must have made the lead story somehow.

"Shocking photos from the local police force show that there wasn't so much as a single blossom on these peach trees a mere two weeks ago," Arlene said in a voice that implied juicy gossip and ghostly tragedy at the same time.

The camera panned to show the orchard, branches sagging under the weight of the glorious ripe peaches.

"The proprietors insist that these trees aren't genetically enhanced, but the results speak for themselves," Arlene said darkly.

"Oh my god, Sage, I'm so sorry—" Arden began.

But Sage was already on her feet, running out the back door to find Tansy.

Her sister was just outside, toweling her hair off from her swim in the pond.

"What's going on, Sage?" Tansy asked.

"When the police were here for the bees, *they took pictures*," Sage said.

"Yeah?" Tansy said.

"And the woman from Channel Eight got a hold of them," Sage said. "She's using the pictures as evidence that the trees bloomed too fast to not be genetically modified."

"No," Tansy said, an expression of despair on her face.

"I know how much you want this farm to work," Sage

said carefully. "I want it to work too. But there's too much going wrong."

"There's nothing that can't be fixed," Tansy said softly.

But Sage could tell from her sister's expression that she was only putting up token resistance. Tansy already knew what was coming.

"I crunched the numbers last night, Tansy," Sage said. "With the new tax bill and the supplies we'll need for next year we just can't make this work - not if we sold every peach on the place."

"I still have money in my account at school—" Tansy began.

"No," Sage said. "We're not touching that again. I wouldn't have let you touch it in the first place if I'd known where you were getting the money."

"It's only money," Tansy said. "I can earn more."

"It's not only money," Sage told her. "How long do you think it will be before someone digs deeper into the operations on this farm? Now that they're suspicious of our practices, we'll be under a microscope."

"The men," Tansy breathed.

"The men," Arden nodded. "I don't know if we can keep them hidden much longer. All we need is for someone to capture them on film and money problems will be the least of our worries."

"So what do we do?" Tansy asked.

"We sell the farm to Dolly and get out of here," Sage said. "You and Arden can take the boys someplace remote. Or split up and take just Burton with you. He might fit in all by himself, and then you can finish school."

"What about you?" Tansy asked.

"I'm going back to work," Sage said. "Someone needs to make some money. I'll help you as best I can."

"What about Riggs?"

Tansy's question hung in the air.

Somehow it hurt too much to think about.

So Sage did what she always did, pressed her emotion deep down and declined to answer.

"He cares about you," Tansy added. "And I know you care about him too."

"Now is a time for action," Sage replied. "Emotions can't play into it."

There was a sound from the other side of the barn.

Sage whipped around, but there was no one there.

"You're doing it again," Tansy said. "You're turning your back on what matters most. When Grandma Helen died, all you could think about was organizing everything, planning the funeral, crunching the numbers."

"Someone has to organize things," Sage said, hurt. "Everyone can't spend all their time saying good-bye. Someone has to make arrangements, or else nothing would ever get done."

Tansy shook her head, eyes wet with unshed tears.

Before Sage could say anything more, Tansy jogged off toward the house.

Sage found herself hoping Burton would find Tansy. He always seemed to be able to make her sister feel better.

She tried not to let herself resent the fact that making Tansy feel better used to be her job.

21

RIGGS

R iggs paced the grassy knoll behind the barn.

He should not have heard what he heard. He'd only been headed to the back door to join the others for dinner. And he'd dashed away as soon as he'd realized he was intruding on a private conversation.

But he was glad he'd overheard a small bit before he rounded the barn.

Sage cared about him, whether she wanted him to know it or not.

And right now she needed his help.

If only he could think of how to help her...

But if what she said was true, it wouldn't matter if he hung up flyers all night. If they had to sell the peaches for more than they were worth, it would not help to bring in a crowd to visit the farm tomorrow.

Her words echoed in his head.

The only thing anyone in this town wants to visit is aliens.

Unfortunately she wasn't wrong. Every time they passed the observatory on the way to town there were crowds outside the hedge. The whole downtown area was full of tourists and souvenir stands. Alien mania was rampant here.

There didn't seem to be as much peach mania.

Suddenly something occurred to him.

He stopped in his tracks, working it out. Surely there was some problem with his logic, some key thing he was missing.

He had taken Sage's comments to heart. He really *had* only been on this planet a short time. His judgment was not equal to the task at hand, at least not yet.

But no matter how he looked at this, it seemed to be an elegant solution.

Quick as a thought, he dashed up the hillside to the peach orchard.

He jogged between the graceful trees. The fruit on the branches was practically bursting it was so ripe. It smelled heavenly.

When he reached the hedge that separated Martin's Bounty from the Observatory, he closed his eyes and called to his brother, Bond.

I need your help brother, he thought as hard as he could. *Please come to me.*

22

SAGE

S age awoke to a pounding on her bedroom door.

"H-hello," she called.

The door flew open. Otis Rogers stood in the threshold, looking as if he had sprinted to her room from the town square.

"Otis, what's going on?" she asked, pulling the sheet around herself so he wouldn't see her skimpy pajamas.

He opened his mouth and closed it again, then shook his head.

"Just get dressed and come out as fast as you can," he said.

"Is something wrong?" she asked, launching herself out of bed as ice water filled her veins. Farms were dangerous places if safety protocol was forgotten for even a moment.

"No," Otis said quickly. "Something's very, very right."

He stepped back into the hallway.

Sage scampered over to the closet grabbed some clothing and dashed to the bathroom to freshen up and dress.

When she came out he was waiting in the hallway.

"The thing is," he said, as if they were already mid-conversation, "it probably wouldn't have been so big, but the first people to arrive put pictures on Instagram."

"Pictures of what?" Sage asked, mystified.

"Well, you'll see," Otis said, walking faster.

He beat her to the front door and held it open.

She stepped out the door and onto the front porch.

Cars filled the gravel lot and spilled onto the lawn.

A line of people stretched from the peach orchard down the drive and out onto the roadway.

And it was barely even light out.

"Good morning," Riggs said from where he stood on the porch. He must have been waiting for her.

"Wow," Sage said, looking out over the crowd at the farm.

"I'll just let you two talk," Otis said, backing into the house.

"Did you make this happen?" Sage asked.

"Not directly," Riggs said. "And it wasn't even my idea. Not really. It was yours."

"What do you mean?" She turned to him, scrutinizing his face.

Riggs smiled down at her.

"Do you remember when you said that if we wanted the farm to earn enough to open again next year that we would need to sell the fruit for twice what it's worth?" he asked.

She nodded.

"The price for fruit-picking today is three times what your grandmother charged," he said.

Sage looked out at the crowd again, amazed.

"Do you remember when you said that the only thing people in this town wanted to see was aliens?" he asked gently.

She nodded and turned slowly to face him again.

"You were right," he said. "I couldn't stop thinking about it. So I talked to my brother last night."

"Your brother?" Sage echoed.

"Yes," Riggs said. "Bond is out there with Posey and baby Estrella Grace. They're going to do a hayride with the kids every two hours today."

"They're here," Sage said.

"Yes," Riggs replied.

"And that's why so many people are here," she said, still trying to get her mind around the idea.

"Correct," he said.

"And the news report, that something is weird about the peaches?" she asked.

"Since my brother is here, everyone assumes that it's some kind of alien magic making the peaches grow," he said. "Now everyone wants Stargazer peaches."

"Stargazer peaches... and they *did* grow fast because of alien magic, so it's not an empty rumor," Sage murmured. "That's... that's... that's brilliant."

"You like the idea?" he asked.

"I love it," she said, wrapping her arms around him and squeezing as tightly as she could.

Happy tears prickled the insides of her eyes and she felt him kiss the top of her head. No matter what her mind told her, she had never experienced anything in her life that felt more right than being in his strong arms.

"Come on," he said gently. "Want to meet them?"

"Yes," she said, her apprehension gone for the first time since she came back to the farm.

They descended the porch steps together, hand in hand.

"We're out of bushel baskets again," Arden yelped,

jogging toward them looking like she'd just run a marathon. "Oh, hi, Sage!"

"Hi," Sage replied. "I'll go grab the spares out of the shed."

"Can you help me hitch the hayride to the tractor?" Arden asked Riggs.

"Sure," he said. "I'll see you in a few minutes," he told Sage.

She smiled up at him and then headed for the old storage shed next to the orchard.

Dozens of families roamed the trees, picking peaches and laughing. Tansy mingled among them, pointing out the best fruit and demonstrating techniques with the picking sticks.

Meanwhile, Bond and Posey and the baby were surrounded by a ring of children who shyly touched Posey's pretty pink dress and capered around to try and amuse baby Estrella Grace.

It was a perfect day, and Sage allowed herself to relax and enjoy the kind of optimism she'd been longing for.

Riggs was right. Everything was going to be just fine.

She hummed to herself as she opened the storage shed.

23

RIGGS

R iggs straightened up from attaching the hayride wagon to the tractor.

Bond and Posey sat in the hay, holding their baby daughter. The wagon was loaded with children, and parents pressed in from both sides, trying to catch a picture of their kids with the alien family.

He stepped forward and out of the way.

Tansy sat on the tractor in front, grinning widely.

"Okay, everyone," Tansy yelled. "Listen up!"

The happy chaos faded to a joyful din.

"These are the safety rules for the hayride," she called out. "Number one, stay seated. Don't get up until we stop. Number two, keep your hands inside the wagon. Number three, have fun!"

The kids cheered and the parents smiled at each other.

Tansy turned the key in the tractor and the engine started right up.

The hayride headed slowly up the hill past the peach orchard.

Tansy pointed to the trees, explaining to the kids about how old they were, and how they had been grown from cuttings of the original trees her grandmother had planted here.

Riggs smiled, realizing Tansy was truly in her element.

He trailed them on foot at a bit of a distance, enjoying the breeze and the sight of all the happy faces.

The tractor looped downhill again, heading for the berry fields, picking up a bit of speed on the way.

Riggs moved closer, covering his eyes against the rising sun to see if Tansy was in trouble. Surely she wouldn't want to go so fast.

At the same moment, he noticed a toddler break away from his mother to get closer to the hayride.

The scene unfolded in a heartbeat.

Tansy was between two lines of tourists waiting to pick berries and the little one was nearly in front of her. There was no place to turn. And the tractor wasn't slowing.

He was not supposed to use his gift in public.

But it wasn't even a decision, not really.

Riggs ran, pushing his muscles until he could feel them burning, and reached the child seconds before impact.

He wrapped his arms around the unsuspecting little one and rolled into the crowd as the tractor smashed into his shoulder.

He could hear Tansy's scream over the terrified shouts of the crowd and the sobs of the toddler in his arms.

He could already feel his shoulder mending, the ligaments tightening back into place.

"Oh my god, oh my god," the child's mother repeated taking him from Riggs. "Thank you."

But Riggs was already turning to see what happened to the runaway hayride.

And now he understood Tansy's frenzied scream.

The tractor and wagon were out of control, hurtling straight at the storage shed by the old berry field.

"Sage," he moaned, running again but knowing that this time he would be too late.

There was a horrible crash as the tractor went straight through the shed and half-ejected itself on the other side, finally coming to a stop as it smashed against a massive oak tree that was just two feet outside the shed.

Smoke billowed from the engine and small flames licked the back of the shed.

Most of the wagon was trapped inside.

Tansy dragged herself off the tractor, yanking the keys from the engine, and staggered toward the side of the shed. She reached it at the same time as Riggs.

Burton arrived by her side a few seconds later.

"We have to get them out," she screamed.

"We will, it's okay, they're going to be okay," he reassured her. "You need to sit down. That was a bad crash."

"The brakes weren't working," Tansy whined, clawing at the side of the shed. "We have to get them out. There are propane tanks stored in there."

Riggs's heart dropped to his stomach.

"I'll call 9-1-1," Tansy said pulling out her phone.

"I'll grab an ax from the barn," Burton added, taking off faster than Riggs had ever seen him move.

A tearing sound came from inside the shed.

A section of wall opened and he could see a small child trying to climb out.

"That's it, there you go," Sage said in a happy way. "Just climb right out."

"I'm here to catch you," Riggs said, tugging on the section of wall until it came loose.

Tourists were wandering down the hill to witness what had happened.

The little girl climbed out into Riggs's arms and he set her down.

She ran down the hill to her father, who swept her up in his arms.

But Riggs focused his attention on the next child, who was already heading his way.

"Sage, you need to look for another opening," he said as calmly as he could, not wanting to frighten the children.

"I can't do that right now," she said lightly. "Here you go!"

Another child came out and another. Some were crying. But more than one was shouting, "Again!" So Riggs figured they were going to be just fine, as long as they could get them all away from the shed before...

"Sage, do you know what is stored in that shed?" he asked.

"I do," she said. "Come on, honey, you can do it."

Another little girl came out, then two boys.

"That's the last of the little ones. Go on, Bond and Posey," Sage said. "I'll come right after you."

Riggs moved aside, and helped his brother down, then his sister-in-law, who held the baby tight to her chest.

"Okay, Sage, now you," Riggs said anxiously, holding his arms out.

"I can't," she said calmly. "I'm pinned to the wall."

"What do you mean you can't?" he howled. The words refused to make sense. "Just push."

"This thing weighs two tons," she told him sensibly. "Even I'm not that determined."

"Tansy is calling 9-1-1," he told her. "Burton is on his way from the barn with an ax."

"Maybe one of them will get me out in time," Sage said, not sounding hopeful. "But I need you to do something for me."

He could hear Tansy in the background telling the tourists to get away from the shed.

"Anything. I'll do anything," he said. "You know that."

"I want you to move away from the shed now," she said softly.

"Sage," he sobbed.

"Listen to that," she whispered.

He quieted his own ragged breath and heard a hissing noise coming from inside.

"One of the propane tanks is leaking," she said. "You need to get to safety.

"No," he cried, tearing helplessly at the wall to the shed. The wood splintered in his hands but he was no closer to getting her out.

"I love you, Riggs," she told him. "I don't want to die without saying it. I wish I could accept you as my mate, and live our lives together in happiness. You are everything to me. But I don't want to imagine a world without you in it. Please move to safety."

"I love you," he told her, moved beyond anything.

"Please," she begged. "Please back away."

Then he felt Burton and Drago's arms around him, dragging him bodily away from the shed. He was too dazed to fight. Too dazed to even think.

They had just reached the edge of the berry field when there was a thunderous explosion.

The air suddenly filled with smoke.

The sound jarred him out of his trance. He broke free from his brothers and ran up the hillside, tears running down his cheeks freely.

Only one wall of the structure still stood. The rest was jagged stone and wood.

When he got close enough to see the true extent of the damage he fell to his knees, burying his head in his hands.

A communal gasp from the gathered crowd made him look up.

From out of the cloud of dust and rubble, a figure emerged.

Tears in his eyes blurred his vision but he could see the long wavy brown hair, and the impeccable posture of his incredible mate, standing in the rubble.

Unharmed.

The remains of her tattered clothing fluttered around her curvy frame as she walked to him, smiling, her eyes shining with tears of her own.

24

RIGGS

F or Riggs, the rest of the day went by in a blur in the aftermath of the accident.

Although Sage had walked out of the rubble unharmed, the ambulance that arrived a moment later insisted on bringing her in. And they wanted to check Riggs out too, since an off-duty EMT who had been peach-picking insisted that he had been hit by the runaway tractor.

Meanwhile at the hospital, Riggs refused medical treatment from the increasingly aggressive staff. He finally made a frantic call to Dr. Bhimani, who asked to be put on the phone with the attending physician. He listened to her for a long time, then hung up and said he understood that Riggs was *under her care*. Thankfully that had the effect of stopping the staff from harassing him and his secret was safe for another day.

Though she appeared to be miraculously uninjured, Sage was kept for observation, with Riggs by her side.

Under the surveillance of the nurses and cameras they could say nothing of their feelings and experiences, so he amused her by reading magazine quizzes out loud to her and roaring with laughter at her answers.

They were finally released just as the sun was sinking. Arden picked them up in the truck. They rode home listening to how the day at the farm had gone, squished pleasantly close by the small cab.

They arrived at home to find Tansy and Burton at the kitchen counter, adding up the day's receipts while Drago pulled a tray of chocolate chip cookies out of the oven.

"Sage," Tansy cried.

"Riggs," Burton said, smiling.

Tansy told them that when the police announced officially that the brakes on the tractor had been sabotaged, social media lit up, and then explained to him and his brothers what most of those words meant when put together like that.

After the announcement, it hadn't taken long for Clement Peterson to turn himself in. Before he did so, he posted a statement:

"I am so sorry. It was just a tractor. I didn't think little kids were going to get involved with it."

Riggs was both relieved and a little disappointed that it had turned out not to be ninjas.

"Oh, so now you're interested in accounting?" Sage teased her little sister, indicating the pile of receipts on the table.

Tansy pushed them over for Sage to peruse for herself.

"Glad you're home, brother," Drago said to Riggs.

"Me too," Riggs agreed. "That was closer than I care to come to disaster."

"But here we are," Drago grinned, his blue eyes flashing.

"Here we are," Riggs had to agree.

"One more weekend like this and we're in the black,"

Sage was telling Tansy over at the counter, her voice soft with wonder.

Tansy wrapped her arms around her sister's neck and squealed.

"We're going to bring cookies over to the observatory," Burton told Riggs quietly. "We have an excuse for a neighborly visit now, to thank Bond and Posey for what they're doing to help the farm. Otis has brought us costumes so we won't be recognized. It will be good to see our brothers."

Riggs nodded, glad they could see their brothers at the observatory, but wondering how long until he could take Sage to bed.

"It will also be good for you to have time alone with your mate," Burton said.

"Alone?" Riggs echoed.

"You're not coming with us," Burton said. "You and Sage need, um, rest."

Riggs looked over at his mate. She glanced up at him as if he had called to her, and smiled.

Riggs smiled back and then nodded to his brother.

"That sounds good," he said.

Sage was already sipping a mug of tea and chatting with Tansy and Arden about how to handle crowd control the next day.

Riggs slipped off and took a shower.

When he came back the others were preparing to leave.

"I'll just take a shower too," Sage said. "My hair is still full of dust."

"Do you want some help?" he suggested.

She blushed and shook her head.

"Should I wait for you in your room?" he asked.

"Yes, please," she whispered, going up on her toes to give

him a quick peck on the cheek that somehow sent his senses reeling.

When his brothers and their mates headed out, Riggs went to Sage's room to wait for her.

He had no intention of rushing her into anything, but he couldn't resist removing his bathrobe and slipping into her bed.

The blanket and pillows carried her light scent. He had a sudden instinct to roll around in it like Cleo the cat did when she found a smell she wanted to keep.

The sound of the shower stopped and he shivered with anticipation.

A moment later, Sage appeared, wrapped in a fluffy white bathrobe.

Riggs sat up.

"Do you feel better?" he asked.

"Yes, the shower felt really good," she replied.

She suddenly looked shy and younger than usual.

He wondered if she was nervous about consummating their mating.

"Come, let me hold you," he offered, holding his arms out. "I'm sure you have a lot of questions about what happened today. It's good that we can talk now."

She smiled and came to him, nestling her warm, fragrant body to his.

The pleasure of it was intoxicating and Riggs felt like he was in a dream, too joyful for it to be real.

"Why didn't I get hurt in the shed?" she asked.

"I think it's the same reason I didn't get hurt when the tractor hit me," he replied carefully.

"So it *did* hit you," she said, her voice tinged with wonder.

"Yes, of course it did," he said. "I felt terrible saying everyone was wrong, but I can't exactly show off my gift."

"So you're super strong?" she asked.

"Not exactly," he said. "I'm... I guess you would say I'm indestructible."

"You're indestructible?" she repeated.

He nodded. "Or unbreakable, however you want to say it."

"That's...that's crazy," she said.

He nodded again.

"But it makes sense," she said. "I remember when you fell off the ladder and you didn't get hurt."

"Yeah," he said. "It was too bad you had to see that."

"Well, it's better now that I know you don't have internal injuries you're hiding," she teased.

He laughed.

"But that doesn't explain why *I* didn't get hurt," she said quietly.

"Oh," he said, trying to think of a way to explain to her that she had chosen to accept him without meaning to.

"I think I know though," she said, shifting around in his arms to face him.

She gazed into his eyes and reached out a tentative hand to stroke his jaw.

"I think it's because I accepted you as my mate," she said.

He closed his eyes against the pleasure of her hand on his skin, her words in his heart.

"Is that what happened?" she asked.

He nodded, unable to speak.

"I'm so glad," she said simply.

And though her words brought him joy, he still had to ask her a question.

"Sage, you said you wished you could be my mate," he

began. "But you thought you were dying and you wanted to protect me. You didn't know you would be held to those words, bound by them."

"And you're worried that I might be sorry?" she asked.

He nodded, searching her face for a sign that he was right.

"I guess I've really been stupid," Sage said, sighing and shaking her head.

"You could never be stupid," he told her.

"That's very sweet of you, Riggs. But honestly, I'm good with numbers and business theory, but not with real things, the things that matter, the things that have been right in front of my eyes," she said.

His heart thundered in his ears.

"I love you," she told him. "I've loved you from the beginning, I think. You're kind and you work hard. You're a good listener. And being with you makes me a better person. I don't think I needed to say those words today for us to be bound. I had already said them in my heart."

He crushed her to his chest, pressing his lips to her hair as she squeezed him back.

"I love you, Sage," he whispered. "I love you so much."

She wiggled out of his hold and put her arms around his neck, hugging him tightly again.

"We don't have to do anything today if you're still getting used to the idea—" Riggs began.

But she slid one hand down to untie her robe.

Suddenly her soft, warm, naked body was pressed to his.

He was nearly overwhelmed by how good it felt to share her body heat, to feel every inch of her with nothing between them.

She pressed her lips to his and he moaned at the sensation.

He ran a hand through her hair and the other down the line of her body, tracing every curve. When he reached her bottom he spread his hand wide and pressed her harder against him.

She whimpered against his mouth and he took the opportunity to deepen the kiss and caress her tongue with his.

Sage clutched his upper arms as if she were trying to hold on.

He understood how she felt. Waves of need swept through him, pushing him to the edge even as he fought to move slowly, and enjoy the experience with her.

When he could bear no more, he pulled away and looked down at her.

Sage gazed up at him, her eyes hazy with need.

"Beautiful," he whispered.

Then he lowered his head to lightly kiss her neck and brush his lips against her collar bone.

She arched her back in invitation.

He nuzzled her generous breasts and licked one stiff little nipple into his mouth.

She moaned lightly in response.

Her sound encouraged him and he skimmed his thumb over the other nipple, teasing it until it was a hard little pebble.

He left one breast to lick and suck at the other.

Sage arched her back as if to beg for more.

Instead, he licked a line down her belly and nudged her thighs open.

Sage stilled and seemed to hold her breath.

Riggs nuzzled her tender inner thighs.

Sage's hips trembled.

He loved to see her respond to his touch, loved the way she allowed him to tease her.

He pressed a kiss to her opening at last and slid his tongue against her, exploring her gently.

"Ohhh," Sage moaned.

The sound went straight to his cock, which went from stiff to throbbing in an instant.

Ignoring the frantic demands of his own body, he licked her slowly and thoroughly, avoiding only the stiff little pyramid he knew would throw her over the edge.

Sage's sounds grew more and more desperate.

When she helplessly lifted her hips to meet his mouth, he knew she was ready.

Giving her one last, loving lick, he crawled up to join her.

She gazed up at him, her eyes luminous, her lips swollen from his kisses.

"Are you ready?" he asked her.

"Yes, please, please," she begged.

25

SAGE

Sage waited, every sense attuned to her mate, as he guided himself against her.

She could feel how wet she was, her whole body opening for him like a peach blossom.

He felt enormous, but she wasn't afraid.

When she lifted her hips to encourage him, he pressed forward, stretching her until she saw stars behind her eyes.

He filled her to bursting.

Sage had never experienced such contentment or such violent lust. She was battered between emotion and desire.

"Sage," he whispered and she saw her own feelings reflected back to her in his eyes.

He was so beautiful, his blue eyes hungry, his jaw tensed as if he were holding himself back.

"Please," she whispered, needing what only he could give her.

He growled and thrust into her again.

Sage moaned and sank her nails into his shoulders.

Riggs groaned and let loose, giving her the powerful thrusts that she craved, filling her again and again.

Sage quivered on the edge, her body straining to contain the pleasure, to endure it without combusting.

Then Riggs slid his hand between them and slowly massaged her stiffened clitoris.

Sage cried out and let go.

She was flying, floating on a sea of a pleasure so intense she could hardly absorb it.

The wave lifted her and then crashed her down in a crushing, blinding agony of ecstasy.

"Sage," Riggs groaned helplessly.

She felt him expand inside her and then he cried out as he filled her with his seed.

The throes of their shared climax seemed to go on forever.

Then Riggs collapsed on her chest, panting.

The room was so still. There was no sound but their breathing.

Sage savored the peace even as she wanted to scream to the world that they were one.

"I can hear your heart," he whispered to her after a while.

"What's it saying?" she asked.

She felt him smile against her chest.

"It wants chocolate chip cookies," he said.

"Riggs," she gave him a gentle smack on the head.

He chuckled and raised his head to look into her eyes.

There was something different about him. He had always had a quiet confidence, but this was something else, a new glow of boldness.

"You're human," she said, realizing it.

"Yes," he said. "Thank you for that."

"Thank me with cookies," she suggested.

He laughed and gathered her in his arms, leaping out of the bed and heading for the door.

"Wait," she laughed. "We need clothes."

He gave her a stormy look but he put her down long enough to grab her robe and toss it to her.

She slid it over her shoulders as he put his on too.

Then they headed out to the kitchen, hand in hand, to begin their life together with two of her favorite things - chocolate chip cookies and plans for the future.

26

RIGGS

R iggs straightened his tie one last time in the bathroom mirror.

He and his brothers were in their room over the barn, preparing for the wedding as the girls got ready in the house. He was reminded suddenly of their first night here, not so long ago.

"I don't think it's going to get much straighter," Drago said kindly, smiling at Riggs in the mirror from over his shoulder.

Riggs turned to see Burton grinning at him from his place by the window in the tackle room.

"Is it time?" Riggs asked.

Drago nodded.

They climbed down the stairs of the old barn and followed the path up to the pond.

The air was cool and fragrant. It was full dark, but fireflies filled the sky, lighting their way.

Now that so much attention was being paid to the home of Stargazer Peaches, they had to be careful about a big event like this one, so they had decided to hold the ceremony after dark.

"Married at midnight, I like it," Sage had said when Tansy suggested the plan for the big wedding.

When Riggs had proposed getting married in the first place, she had only sobbed like a child and hugged him so hard it would have broken a lesser man's ribs.

And now it was about to happen.

From what he had been given to believe about Earth's wedding customs, their plan was exceedingly simple.

But that didn't mean the whole farm hadn't been exploding with wedding activity.

Otis, whose passion for baking had recently become a farm attraction, ceased peach pie production temporarily to concoct a presumably incredible wedding cake, which no one was allowed to see until the big event.

The pie stand he'd set up at the newly busy farm was bringing in enough money that Sage had insisted on putting him on payroll.

"I won't take your money," he said.

"I insist," Sage retorted, a gleam of a threat in her eyes.

"I'll spend it all on wedding cake ingredients," he countered, taking the check she pushed into his hands and scurrying away before she could argue.

Tonight they would see what he had been working on.

Meanwhile, Tansy and Burton had been spending early mornings weeding and planting around the pond. And Drago and Arden stopped by each evening to encourage the new life to grow.

No one else was allowed near the pond. Which made Riggs a little grumpy.

Sage, being the practical one, planned out the ceremony

and created the invitations, such as they were, with Riggs's help.

"No one is coming besides us," Riggs had said, confused.

"Oh, it's nice to have something to commemorate the day," she had replied with a secret smile.

So many secrets.

Like the one in his pocket.

On the day of their escape, Dr. Bhimani had given the men an envelope of cash to be used in case of an emergency. They'd had a private meeting this week and decided that a proper wedding for their mates qualified.

Without the women knowing, the three brothers had made an extra stop on their trip to town last week to purchase three slender gold rings and three plain silver ones from the local jewelry shop. Their marriages would have all the trappings.

They had reached the pond at last.

Otis sat on a stool near the water, playing *Greensleeves* softly on his ukulele.

In the darkness, Riggs could see that the tall grasses and shrubs that surrounded the north side of the pond were gone and something smaller was in their place. The delicate fragrance of flowers floated on the breeze.

"Roses," Burton whispered.

"It is beautiful, brothers, well done," Riggs whispered back.

Burton nodded, looking pleased.

The flickering of candlelight came from the other side of the pond.

"They're here," Drago breathed.

The rest of it seemed to go in slow motion.

Arden appeared first, wearing a simple white cotton dress that was a perfect contrast to her dark hair, in which she wore a circlet of flowers. She smiled up at Drago as he came to take her hand.

Then Tansy arrived, even taller than normal in high-heeled sandals and a silvery dress that revealed her shoulders. Her short hair was glossier than usual and shimmering earrings skimmed her collarbones. Burton ran to take her hand, earning her indulgent smile.

At last Sage walked slowly around the pond to the rhythm of the music. Her wavy hair was down around her back and she wore a long, lace dress that made Riggs think of tiny stars against a sky. It was old-fashioned yet beautiful, just like his darling mate. And Riggs felt a love so fierce it was like a pain in his chest.

When her hand was at last in his, he nearly cried with relief.

"We have a surprise for you," Sage told him.

The hedges on the south side of the pond were suddenly *moving.*

He realized that in the darkness his eyes had been fooled. Two screens with branches on them had stood in for the shrubbery.

Behind them were seven smiling people, each holding a candle, except for the one holding the baby.

Bond and Posey, Rocky and Georgia, Rima and Magnum, and Dr. Bhimani, with baby Estrella Grace in her arms, all faced them smiling.

"Guests," Riggs breathed.

"Guests," Sage agreed, squeezing his hand.

And now he knew why they had hand printed the beautiful invitations.

There was a flurry of excited whispering and waving, and then the ceremony began.

The words washed over him and he managed to follow along, but Riggs was lost in a sea of love and wonder.

At the proper moment he slid the ring onto Sage's finger and was gratified by her expression of surprise and delight.

Then he was bending to kiss her, pressing his lips to hers as if they could somehow freeze the moment if only he kissed her thoroughly enough.

When they finally broke apart, the guests cheered.

They all followed the path back down to the barn where Otis had set up their reception.

The interior of the barn was aglow with fairy lights.

Three enormous cakes covered the large table in the middle.

"There's one for each couple, so everyone has to eat three pieces," Otis announced.

Arden and Drago's cake was carrot with cream cheese frosting and a garnish of peach blossoms on top.

Tansy and Burton's was a honey cake, festooned with hundreds of delicate marzipan bees.

And the cake for Sage and Riggs was a traditional vanilla wedding cake with peach infused frosting and a constellation of chocolate chips on top.

Music started in the background and Riggs wondered if they would dance soon.

"Is that David Bowie?" Sage asked Rima, who had come over to congratulate them.

"Oh, yes," Rima laughed. "That's my mom's old *Heroes* album. It's the only one we have on cassette tape. Otis called in a panic earlier and said there was no music in the barn. The boom box is the only thing we had with a big speaker that runs on batteries. Sorry."

"No," Sage told her. "Don't be sorry. I think... I think it's just right."

"Shall we dance?" Riggs asked her.

"Do you know how?" she asked.

"My training was watching 80s movies, of course I do" he teased her. "You're a silly girl for asking that question."

She grinned and he swept her into his arms.

Over her shoulder, he could see his brothers and their mates on the dance floor, beginning to sway under the fairy lights.

Outside this barn, he knew, were the rest of the humans who inhabited the surface of this wild, sad, funny, inexplicable planet.

He was truly one of billions of brothers and sisters now - a full-fledged participant in Earth's chaotic march toward who knew what ends - tragic or magical. This was a brotherhood so much larger than himself and those he loved, that he was humbled by it and overwhelmed with a desire to help them all somehow.

But for tonight, he turned his attention back to his own mate, and the sweet universe that was her love.

Sage lifted her chin to meet his eyes, as if knowing he was dreaming again, worrying about a world so big he could hardly change it in a hundred lifetimes.

He waited to see what she would say, yearning to hear her thoughts and feelings on this important evening as they began their life together formally.

But she only smiled up at him. It was a smile that told him that all was well, that she was his and he was hers. It was her most twinkly-eyed smile, the one that brought him back to himself as he realized she always would.

He smiled down at her, amazed that he had found her, amazed that she had accepted him - accepted everything about him.

And they whirled to the music as the blue-green planet whirled around its only star, joyfully, steadily, forevermore.

***

Thanks for reading Riggs!
Keep reading for a sample of a NEW Stargazer Alien series:
Tolstoy: Stargazer Alien Barbarian Brides.

Or grab your next book right now:
http://www.tashablack.com/stargazer.html

TOLSTOY (SAMPLE)

1

ANNA

I n a forgotten corner of the galaxy, far from the established trade routes, and even farther from where it was supposed to be, floated a long-forgotten ship, one among many.

And at the center of that abandoned ship grew a forest.

Anna Nilsson froze in place, wishing there were someone to share the unusual sight with her. But she was alone, the only sound the hiss of the air pump in her spacesuit.

She stepped closer, mesmerized.

After the endless burnished aluminum of the *Stargazer*, the lush greenery before her almost hurt to look at.

Anna stood in a derelict luxury star cruiser the size of a shopping mall. She'd already made her way through winding corridors of threadbare rugs and corroded, flickering chandeliers, using her tagger to mark items of interest along the way. The passageways circled rings of rooms that extended along the sides of the ship as far as she could see. She almost felt as if she were in a *Scooby Doo* episode, or visiting the sunken Titanic, until she opened the latest door.

Maybe it was the lack of sleep since she'd found out she would be running her first salvage mission completely solo, or maybe the oxygen mix in her suit was a little high, but Anna couldn't shake the feeling she'd stepped into a dream. She blinked to clear her head, but nothing changed.

She stood before a huge wall of glass, or something like glass, anyway. Beyond the wall, trees - real, honest to god trees - stretched upward, their lumpy branches bristling with bright green leaves. They had to be hundreds of years old.

As a child, Anna had visited the indoor rain forest exhibit at the Baltimore Aquarium on Earth. Clutching her big brother's hand, she'd dashed up the wooden platforms, trying to catch a glimpse of the sloth or the toucan. The trees there had been spread out, the bustling city always looming just outside the floor-to-ceiling windows.

What stood before her now was not an engineered approximation. It was a real forest, branches growing thick enough to block out the light source above. The surreal scene was made complete by a pair of ancient looking lamp posts glowing faintly at the edge of the tree line, their light barely penetrating a few steps into the wooded area.

The ship was as good as dead, but the forest was very much alive. Tendrils of ivy burst through the crevices between the corroded metal panels that held the glass in place, refusing to bend to the will of the man-made structure.

Hot tears sprung to her eyes and Anna had to lean over and rest her hands on her knees to steady herself in the wake of sudden emotion.

She hadn't seen a tree in six months.

Well, technically it had been far, far longer. But she tried not to think about that part.

Light from above filtered down into the woods, dappling the soil and stones beneath the trees.

For a moment Anna was back at the cafe in Tarker's Hollow, gazing out the window at the park as her mother scolded her to bus the lunch tables. She could smell the almond croissants baking, hear the mindless chatter of the patrons as they discussed whatever it was people with real lives discussed. It had been her entire existence, and now it was just... gone.

A light breeze sent a shiver of motion through the leaves in front of her. It must have been manufactured weather, still operating on reserve energy. The movement highlighted what she hadn't noticed before.

The plant life had run riot, but there were no birds, no squirrels, not even insects on the forest floor. Besides Anna, the forest was the only living thing on the ship.

She stepped closer, placed her gloved hand against the nearest pane in solidarity, and holstered her tagger. She couldn't imagine needing it in here.

A tremendous sycamore towered over her head just inside the glass.

She gazed up into its branches. The light seemed to be brightening above.

No. That wasn't right.

The tree was brightening.

Before her eyes, the green leaves faded then burst into flaming orange.

All around the sycamore the other trees erupted into a symphony of yellow, peach, pink and scarlet.

Anna was watching summer turn to fall, as if someone had pressed a button on the remote that controlled the speed of the world.

A tone sounded in her helmet.

She looked down at her wrist.

Her origami drone unfolded from its dock and then refolded itself into something resembling a bird, before fluttering up to her.

"The atmosphere is breathable," BFF19 sang out.

Anna released her helmet and pulled it off.

***

Thanks for reading this sample of Tolstoy!
Grab the rest of the story now:
www.tashablack.com/sabb

TASHA BLACK STARTER LIBRARY

Packed with steamy shifters, mischievous magic, billionaire superheroes, and plenty of HEAT, the Tasha Black Starter Library is the perfect way to dive into Tasha's unique brand of Romance with Bite!

Get your FREE books now at tashablack.com!

ABOUT THE AUTHOR

Tasha Black lives in a big old Victorian in a tiny college town. She loves reading anything she can get her hands on, writing paranormal romance, and sipping pumpkin spice lattes.

Get all the latest info, and claim your FREE Tasha Black Starter Library at www.TashaBlack.com

Plus you'll get the chance for sneak peeks of upcoming titles and other cool stuff!

Keep in touch...
www.tashablack.com
authortashablack@gmail.com

facebook.com/romancewithbite

twitter.com/romancewithbite